ANANT DOTCOM

ANANT DOTCOM

A Novel

Dr. Govind Sharma

PARTRIDGE

To order additional copies of this book, contact
Partridge India
000 800 10062 62
orders.india@partridgepublishing.com

www.partridgepublishing.com/india

Prologue

I was sitting in verandaha of my friend's house at Hardoi. I was on a visit to Hardoi District to preach about Ram Charit Manas.

My pravachan (a religious speech) would start after half an hour. My friend's son Vinayak brought a copy of Amar Ujala newspaper; I flipped through its pages.

On the third page, I came across an interesting advertisement about a website where someone was offering advice to young boys and girls about Sports.

"Do you have everything except the opportunity? Do you have talent but no one to appreciate it? Is your hidden potential waiting to be unleashed? We will transform your dreams to your destiny. Your rightful place is at the top in the Sports World and we will help you reach there. Don't just sit there wondering what to do next. Please click our website. Boys and Girls, please log on to Anant dotcom and register free of charge."

Could it be my friend Anant? I had not heard from him for quite some time; his whereabouts were not known for last so many years. The newspaper ad only gave the web address.

When I logged the website, I could not get names and addresses of those who ran the website. The advice was being offered only through email. Those making queries were referred to Training Institutions, given information about Sports Scholarships, or provided with fitness tips. It appeared that the website was managed by a single person.

After my Hardoi visit, I tried very hard to find Anant. I made phone calls, sent text messages and emails; I even used private detectives. But my search was in vain. Anant remained only a website.

I also instituted enquiries about the physical location of the website but I was told that in the modern era of cloud technology, it is very difficult to trace the location by website.

I web searched the relevant details, but all I got was a clutter of mixed information.

I went to the biggest library and went through papers and magazines of the period when Anant had gone missing. There was nothing to suggest where Anant might have gone. But there were some stories about enquiries by the Income Tax Department against some Sports Bodies.

I met Karan, Joint Commissioner Income Tax in Delhi, who was in College with me and Anant.

'I have no information about Anant.' He said

'Anant is not associated with the Sports Bodies whose accounts were investigated.' He added.

'Who all are involved?' I got curious.

'We cannot say anything without hard evidence and conclusive proof.' Karan spoke in officialese.

'But tongues have been wagging.' I said.

'You cannot base your judgment on the malicious hearsay.' He asserted.

'Fine, but you should inform me if you come to know about Anant's whereabouts.' I requested him.

'Of Course, I will. After all, you were his friend, philosopher, and guide in the College.' Karan said.

My thoughts took me down the memory lane to the time when I was in College.

Part I

Dharampur

Chapter 1

It all began in my Second Year in Saint John's College. It is a low profile College in Dharampur, a small town in foot hills of Shivalik about 50 kilo meters from Chandigarh.

Anant came from a big business family, but he had to shift from a very high profile College in Mumbai to my College because he had fallen in bad company.

I was obliged to be in Anant's company because our grandfathers came from the same place, a small village in Rajasthan. They even studied together for a few years. Both the families worshipped Salasar Hanumanji.

Anant's grandfather became a big businessman with net-worth in thousands of crores. My grandfather belonged to a family of priests and he became a kathavachak (a preacher reciting scriptures).

My father studied in gurukul (a traditional Indian school) and started helping my grandfather in kathavachan. But when it came to the grandchildren, my grandfather wanted to expose us to the western education system in Public School and College. He believed that those with the traditional background should be familiar with the modern thought process, and the westernized Indians should take interest in the ancient Indian teachings so as to have a balanced outlook on life.

I was staying in College Hostel as my family was in Delhi.

Anant's grandfather suggested that Anant should stay with me as I would be a good influence on him because of my religious upbringing. My grandfather agreed. He saw only good in people. Moreover, he was certain that I will not learn bad habits from Anant as he thought my moral fiber was very strong.

Anant's family rented a two room accommodation with kitchen, about half a kilometer from our College. I was very happy to shift from Hostel to Digs (as Anant called the rented accommodation). It was a complete package as Anant's family arranged for a cook, a cleaner cum housekeeper, and a driver.

- - - - - -

Chapter II

I tried hard to concentrate on my book on History of Indian Culture and Civilization. Our quarterly tests had just begun; I did well in that day's test and was preparing for the next day, but I was being distracted by what Anant was doing.

Anant was sitting on a muddha (a small chair made of cane) with a bottle of beer placed on a small table in front of him. His new friend Panther was giving him company. There was a pack of 555 cigarettes on the table.

'How was the test? Pal.' Panther asked.

Anant did not answer.

Champa, the cook, brought a plate of pakodas. Anant picked one and began to nibble. Then he answered Panther's query.

"It was a stupid test. I did not write a word in the answer book. The invigilator got furious when I lit a cigarette, and he asked me to leave the Examination Hall. I came out in fresh air, which was a much better thing to do instead of wasting time in answering stupid questions set by Verma."

Verma Sir taught us General Studies; he was also our Sports Teacher.

I was shocked. I knew Anant had left the test halfway; I could not believe he was asked to leave the Exam because he was smoking. The invigilator was sure to complain to the Principal.

Pan Singh Tharad alias Panther was studying in the nearby Government College called Dharampur College. He was about three years older than us, but still stuck in the Second Year of BA. He met Anant at a Sports Meet, and they became friends because Panther never disagreed with what Anant said. That was the main quality Anant sought in a friend; if Anant found a yes man, he ignored all his faults.

'Let Mohan study. He is a scholar'. Panther said.

'I am fine.' I said.

'The College is not so bad, but I hate Math and I cannot do any paperwork. I think the paperwork is for Munims (clerks).' Anant said.

Champa came in to add more pakodas to the platter. She was hardly twenty; her husband Raju who served as driver was almost twice her age as it was his second marriage.

Panther looked at Champa in a lecherous manner, but did not say anything.

Panther turned to Anant.

'I am more interested in the real book.'

'What would that be?' Anant asked.

'I mean the one that is kept by a bookie. I have already made five grand on Indian Cricket Team's last tour.' Panther elaborated.

'I do not like betting. I like Cricket but I rate it after Soccer and Tennis. If I have my way with Cricket, I would like to liberate the game from the shackles of moronic Cricket Administrators.' Anant said.

'Some day you will! You have all that it takes.' Panther said.

'You are right. If I set my sights on something, nobody can check me from getting there.' Anant said.

'Best of luck! Pal! I have limited ambitions of being successful in betting on Indian Cricket Team's next tour. Panther said.

'I did not know you were so much into betting. I hate betting!' Anant said

'How good you are at it?' Anant asked.

'You have no idea!' Panther said, and left throwing a meaningful glance towards the kitchen.

- - - - - -

Chapter III

'You will be sent home! I do not care that you come from such a big family.'

Verma Sir was admonishing Anant. He was very unhappy with Anant's behavior during the test.

Anant and I kept quiet.

Anant had been summoned by Verma Sir. I accompanied him to give him moral support, and also because of the notion that my nice and clean boy image would render the reprimand less severe.

'I will report the matter to the Principal.' Verma Sir said.

'This shall not happen again Sir.' I said.

'You keep quite. You are not his Guardian. Let him speak.' Verma Sir said.

'Sorry Sir.' Anant said.

'Sorry is not enough.' Verma Sir said. He was of sanctimonious temperament.

I realized time had come to change the topic.

'Sir we would like to seek your guidance about the coming Sports and Cultural Meet.'

I was referring to the forthcoming Inter College Sports and Cultural meet to be held in about ten days. Verma Sir was the organizer in chief of this event which was held every year in our College. All Colleges of Dharampur and some Colleges from the nearby places participated in Sports, Cultural, and Literary events.

'Sir, I would like to participate in Debate Competition and Anant in Drama.'

My strategy appeared to work as Verma Sir simmered down, and wanted to know how well prepared we were for the events.

Anant managed to annoy Verma Sir once again.

'Debate and Drama are alright, but our Sports Grounds are in a mess. They look like a Municipal Dump Yard, and the Dressing Room is like a Cow Shed.' Anant said.

Anant wasn't far removed from truth; but as Verma Sir was in charge of Sports and Cultural activities, he took umbrage to Anant's remarks. It reflected on his initiative and supervisory abilities.

'We will see if we have Cow Sheds or Pig Sties.' Verma Sir glowered at Anant.

Our meeting with Verma Sir ended when his nine year old son Bunty came looking for him.

Anant's Cow Shed remark made it more or less certain that he would be summoned by the Principal.

- - - - - -

Chapter IV

Sudha joined our class in August, and improved the glamour index of our College by several points. Her father was an Army Officer who had recently been posted to Chandigarh, which was a very lucky break for the boys of our class. There were other girls too, but Sudha immediately occupied the position of the queen superior.

Sudha was tall, fair and sharp featured with a model's figure. She had airs of a princess and manners of a diplomat. All the boys of our college immediately fell in love with her. If she happened to drop her pen in the class, about fifteen boys competed with each other to restore the pen to her. As some of my friends confided, she was the chief object of their fantasies.

Sudha was aware of her appeal but kept herself aloof. This added to her aura, and she became the most desirable but unattainable princess. She could have been easily elected President of our College, if ever there was such an election.

Mala was one classmate who was not happy with Sudha's arrival because the attention of the boys shifted from her to Sudha. Mala was also a beautiful girl, but Sudha scored over her.

Mala was affable and loquacious which made her very popular with the boys, but now most of her friends secretly yearned for Sudha. As far as Anant was concerned, it was only a matter of time before he threw his charm around to impress Sudha.

Anant could not be a secret admirer as he was very confident and aggressive. Besides, there was this thing about him knowing his mind and getting what he wanted.

I was standing with Anant when we saw about a dozen boys following Sudha, who was walking gracefully towards the Notice Board. The boys were vying with each other to get her attention, but Sudha ignored them completely.

"Let the mice play; the cat will come, and take the ball away." Anant said after watching the scene for a while.

I ignored Anant's comment, and waived at Vijay who was walking towards the Library.

Vijay was the only one who was not affected by Sudha's admission to our College. He was a typical one woman man. He had already given his heart to Shweta, and did not waste his time in running after other girls. He spent most of his time studying because of which we called him a book worm.

- - - - - -

Chapter V

I and Anant were in the library searching books in the Plays section. Anant wanted to do Romeo's role in the Play Romeo & Juliette.

Though Anant hadn't told me, it was an easy guess that he was going to ask Sudha to play the role of Juliette. If Anant decided to do something, nobody could stop him. We finally got a version of the Play that could be enacted in about forty minutes.

Now we had to convince Sudha to play Juliette; I was sent by Anant to her house in Chandigarh to plead with her parents.

Reluctantly, I went to Colonel Baxi's House. I always felt very nervous when in presence of the Military Officers. It was good that I had sought an appointment in writing by mailing a request three days ago.

'Sir, I have come to request you to permit Sudha to play Juliette in a Play we are staging in the Inter College Meet.' I set the ball rolling.

'Have you asked Sudha?' Colonel Baxi asked.

'No Sir, I would speak with her only after your approval.'

My polite approach did the trick.

'All Right! Who is playing Romeo?' Colonel Baxi wanted to know.

'My friend Anant will play the part, Sir.' I replied.

'Where do you figure?' Colonel Baxi asked.

'I am directing the Play.' I replied

"I will talk to Sudha and she will convey my decision to you.' Colonel Baxi said.

There was nothing left for me except to seek Colonel's permission to leave.

- - - - - -

Chapter VI

We were required to broach the subject to Sudha; Anant insisted that I should request her formally to play Juliette, and he would take over if Sudha acted pricey.

I spotted Sudha coming out of the library; she was moving towards the canteen.

'Hello, Sudha.' I said.

'Hi, Mohan! I heard your speech about Ram Charit Manas the other day. It was superb!' She was in good mood.

She was referring to the elocution contest held in Dharampur Town Hall about origin of religions. I had spoken in detail about why Ram Charit Manas was written; the basic material had been mailed by my grandfather. I had plans to make another appearance next month in Ambala Town Hall from where I had got an invite to speak in a symposium on Indian religions.

'Can I treat you to a cup of Coffee?' I said.

'Why? What is the occasion?' she asked.

'I wonder if we could interest you in playing Juliette in a Play we are planning to stage in the Inter College Meet.' I came to the point.

"What do you mean by 'we'?' she asked.

'Anant and I.' I said.

'He will act as Romeo and I will direct the Play.' I added as we sat down in the canteen.

'Oh! No wonder!' Sudha said.

'How do you mean 'no wonder'?' This was my turn to seek clarification.

'Anant has been staring at me for last so many days. Now in the second stage of his foul schemes, you have been roped in.' She replied.

'I do not like Anant because his behavior is so outrageous; he was smoking in the class during the quarterly test'. She added.

I realized it was very difficult to defend Anant; I had to change my approach.

'It is not so much as his friend that I am approaching you. Mainly, I feel that the role of Juliette is tailor made for you'. I said

'And you think Romeo is tailor made for Anant.' She snapped.

'He is the best I can get. You know the options are very limited.' I said realizing how diplomatic one can become in a difficult situation.

'What experience do you have of directing Plays?' She asked.

'Not much. I did it only twice. Once it was a Hindi Play. The other time I tried directing Anton Chekhov's Play 'The Bear' which was a very ambitious thing to do, so it had to be aborted halfway.' I said.

'Please tell me more about it.' Sudha was getting interested.

'The heroin could not memorize Papova's dialogues, and the boy playing Luka fell ill.' I said.

'I will think about your offer.' Sudha said while getting up.

'If Anant survives today's meeting with the Principal, that is.' She added.

There were no secrets in our College.

- - - - - -

Chapter VII

I came across Anant in the front Courtyard. His gleaming face indicated that his meeting with the Principal was alright, and that Verma Sir's complaint was ignored. May be his powerful industrialist father intervened.

'My Mamaji's phone did the trick. I am not getting thrown out of the College.' Anant said.

Anant's Mamaji (Maternal Uncle) was a very influential person. His sphere of influence included politicians, bureaucrats, film persons, media barons and above all the corporate houses. There were some controversies linked to him and sometimes his methods were questionable, but he was a Samaritan at heart.

Also, if there was one person in the world who could change Anant's mind it was his Mamaji.

'How was it with Sudha?' Anant asked.

'She is acting tough. But eventually she will agree.' I replied.

'Atta boy!' Anant said.

Our conversation ended when we saw Mala coming towards us with Verma Sir's son Bunty, who was looking very pleased with his hands full of chocolates and popcorn. It was Mala's policy to keep the children of faculty members in good humor.

Chapter VIII

Next day I gave a copy of the script to Sudha. She turned out to be a keen type, as she memorized her dialogues in just two days.

The main problem was Anant. You cannot live on confidence alone; there are times when you have to toil, but Anant was not meant for slog. He managed through sheer confidence and optimism. This worked on most occasions, but in order to perform in a Play one had to make serious efforts.

Soon I realized we will require a very efficient prompter behind the curtain.

For prompter, our classmate Karan appeared to be the perfect choice; he was highly disciplined and had scholarly aptitude. Karan agreed to my request to be the main prompter, and that was half the battle.

Now we had to arrange for the costumes. I was planning to visit Chandigarh with Anant and Sudha to get the costumes stitched; Sudha's mother would help us in finding the right material, and take us to the right tailor.

Anant had different ideas.

'Let us go to Mumbai, Man! I am not going to wear costumes stitched in a small town.' He said

'How can Sudha go to Mumbai?' I said

'Let us ask for her measurements and we will get readymade costumes for her from Mumbai.' Anant had answer for every question.

Sudha declined Anant's offer. So it was decided that she will visit Chandigarh on Sunday, and arrange for her costumes.

- - - - - -

Chapter IX

Sudha was walking through sector 17 market when she realized she was being followed. Being an Army Man's daughter, she was not afraid of such situations but she felt uneasy. Two ruffians around 25 years in age, dressed in loud and garish clothes, were following her. She had never seen these men before; their manner was furtive and annoying.

One of the goons was wearing red shirt and blue scarf; the other one wore military green T shirt with yellow scarf and a thick golden chain. Sudha contemplated about confronting them, but wiser counsels prevailed. She went into a show room to select material for her costume.

To her chagrin, the goons also entered the show room.

Sudha decided to mind her own business. She guessed the goons were just following her. Apparently, they meant no harm; but they were certainly getting on her nerves.

Quietly, she selected the dress material and walked out of the show room. While coming out of the show room she came across Baldev, a classmate of ours.

Baldev was disheveled, and was reeking of alcohol.

'I saw two persons following you. Were they bothering you?' Baldev asked Sudha.

'Oh, No. Not much. Thanks anyway.' She replied.

Baldev was an emotional wreck who came from a dysfunctional family. His father was an idealist who, against his father's wishes, married an orphan; Baldev's grandfather never forgave his son for this act of defiance. Baldev's mother was an alcoholic and a drug addict, and she had been to jail thrice.

Though Baldev was highly talented and creative, he shunned hard work. For him, the inner world inside his heart was more important than the duties and requirements of the outer world. He was a typical example of escapism coupled with self- destruction. At a very early age, he developed all possible bad habits.

He was interested in poetry and drama. Though he was very good at creative arts, he lacked consistency and he spent most of his time drinking and day dreaming.

Baldev took a liking to Sudha which soon turned into obsession; she was the ultimate goddess in his fantasies.

Baldev had followed Sudha all the way from Dharampur to Chandigarh. He wanted to speak to her, but his nerves deserted him. So he went into a bar to soothe his nerves wondering if he could speak to Sudha after consuming alcohol. After the second peg, he spotted Sudha entering a posh show room opposite the bar. Sudha was being followed by two unpleasant looking guys.

Baldev got an impulse that he should protect Sudha. He came out of the bar, and started walking towards the show room. Hardly had he reached the entrance of the show room, when Sudha came out.

Baldev did not know what to say beyond asking her if those guys pestered her.

Vaguely, he offered to escort her to her house.

Sudha politely refused. Baldev's scrawny appearance did not inspire much confidence.

Baldev was a high-strung, dreamy suitor who was drawn to Sudha like the proverbial moth to flame; but he was not able to work on his inadequacies.

That was the story of Baldev's life: he wanted to be the center of attraction, but did not know how to go about it; and had no intentions of working for it, even if he knew how to go about it.

Sudha called an auto rickshaw and said bye to Baldev.

Chapter X

Anant finished his third beer.

Anant had taken me to Panther's room for a friendly party. Since I did not touch alcohol, I was getting thoroughly bored.

Four criminal looking guys were also there, in the capacity of Panther's close friends.

Panther lived in a one room accommodation in a building having about twenty one/two room sets. The building was situated just behind Dharampur Civil Hospital; a number of nurses and paramedics also lived in those rooms.

Panther was a nuisance as he frequently misbehaved with the nurses; they complained against him to the landlord, but he did not have the courage to evict him.

Panther was particularly after Nurse Merry Kutty, a beautiful girl in her early twenties.

That evening, Panther had called his friends and Anant for a party.

'We gave a scare to your darling in sector 17.' One of Panther's friends said looking towards Anant.

'You have got a hot one.' Friend number two said.

I was astounded to know that Anant had set goons after Sudha so that she gets scared, and then he can impress her at the right time by playing gallant.

Only Anant could do this, I thought.

Soon the discussion turned to the physical attributes of Sudha. Panther's friends were getting overboard which was too much; as a result, Anant got upset.

I pacified all concerned and prevented a fight.

The peace was short lived.

Panther, who had gone out of the room for a short while, came back in a disheveled condition.

His shirt was torn and he had a black eye.

'What happened?' we asked in unison.

'Oh it is nothing. Panther said.

We all heard a loud knock at the door and some angry voices outside the room.

I went to open the door since I was the only one sober.

There were three extremely angry looking men standing at the door. One of them was holding a knife. He threatened to kill Panther.

Panther hid behind his friends.

One of Panther's friends came up, and started yelling at the visitors. Friend number two broke an empty beer bottle, and came ahead to face the man with knife. I stopped him and tried to engage the visitors in conversation.

They were furious as Panther had knocked at the door of Nurse Merry Kutty, and when she opened the door he misbehaved with her. Merry Kutty's brother, who was on a short visit to be with his sister, went to the neighbors and told them about Panther's intrusion. They all got agitated, and wanted to teach Panther a lesson.

One of the neighbors, who had a soft corner for Merry Kutty, wanted to express himself more with his knife than with his words. Panther's friend had plans to match his knife with a broken beer bottle. I saved the dual in the nick of the time.

I apologized on behalf of all, and the gentlemen left for their rooms with the warning that should this happen again they would go to the Police. The gentleman holding knife reminded us of his resolve to kill Panther.

Instead of apologizing for the unpleasantness he had put us through, Panther was boasting about his chances with Merry Kutty; and that how soon she will start dancing to his tunes. One of his friends, who was a bus conductor, announced his plan to park a fleet of buses outside the building the next day; which would prevent Merry Kutty and her friends from going out of the building.

On our way back, I took Anant to task asking him why he was friendly with a scum like Panther.

'I value friendship more than anything else. You have to ignore their faults, and help them when they are in trouble. That's how you win their loyalty.' Anant said.

I found it difficult to reconcile to his line of arguments. Anant was not able to discern between friends and sycophants.

I changed the topic of conversation and drew Anant's attention towards the forthcoming Play Romeo & Juliette in which he was to play the lead.

'Have you memorized your lines?' I asked him.

'Boy! I have got terrific costumes made for me; I am going to look the part. Have you found the right costume for Sudha?'

Obviously, Anant cared more about the costumes than his lines.

The news of Sudha doing Romeo &Juliette, that too with Anant, did not go well with Mala. She was not the one to miss any important event. She started planning for action.

Chapter XI

I went to see 3 pm show of a movie in the local cinema theater with Baldev and Karan. Mala was also there along with our two classmates, Neelu and Garima.

Mala was looking stunning in Jeans and T Shirt; she always dressed with panache.

Mala, Neelu, and Garima sat three rows behind us.

We were pleasantly surprised in the interval when Mala came to our row and offered us a packet of peanuts.

'Hi, Baldev!' She threw her charm at him, more or less ignoring me and Karan.

As Baldev had not ingested any alcohol since lunch, he was sober enough to return Mala's greetings. But he was as surprised as me and Karan on Mala's initiative.

'Enjoying the movie?' She said.

'Yes, it is a great movie!' Karan replied on behalf of three of us.

I did not feel like contributing much to the conversation and Baldev was too taken aback to say anything. Moreover, as the interval was about to end, Mala had to go back to her seat.

'See you Baldev!' Mala supplied a booster dose of her charm, and moved towards her seat.

This exclusive attention to Baldev was too much for us to take in. Mala must be having something to work on Baldev. As we came to know later, Mala wanted Baldev to do a Play for her.

- - - - - -

I and Karan were waiting in the canteen for Baldev, who had gone out for a walk with Mala.

Baldev had very reluctantly accepted Mala's offer for a walk with her. He was worried that he would ruin his chances with Sudha if he was seen walking with Mala. He tried to avoid her but one evening Mala buttonholed him, and he was left with no choice but to listen to her.

Our wait ended after half an hour when Baldev showed up looking like he had been robbed. He had a quarter of whisky stuffed in his pocket.

'She wants me to stage a Play in the forthcoming event.' He said lighting a cigarette.

Karan objected to Baldev's smoking.

'If you want me to continue our friendship, you will have to quit smoking.' Karan said.

Baldev, like always, said that was his last cigarette.

'What Play you have in mind?' I asked.

'In such a short time, I can only stage Devdas which I have done thrice.' Baldev replied.

There was no question about Baldev's ability to play Devdas. He had just to be himself. But Mala was not likely to be very convincing as Paro.

'I agreed on the condition that, after the Play, Mala will plead my case with Sudha.' Baldev said.

'I would have no such hopes from Mala. She appears to like you. Why should she encourage the competition?' I said.

- - - - - -

Chapter XII

The Drama Contest was going to be a mega event as both the beauty queens of our College were participating.

My immediate problem was to prepare Anant for the Play.

Anant was a director's nightmare. He was not taking any interest in the rehearsals.

Shakespeare had described Romeo as bearing himself as a portly (stately) gentleman, who was known as a virtuous and well governed youth. Anant was certainly a gentleman, but it was very difficult for a director to make him attend the rehearsals.

Karan as a prompter had a tough task cut out for him.

Karan worked very hard without complaining; he was always like that.

Like me, Karan also came from a religious family. His parents lived in Talwandi Sabo, a place near Bathinda, which is a place of great religious significance as it is one of the five Sikh Takhats.

Karan was indefatigable. Apart from prompting, he shared the burden of direction, and did most of the production work as well. He was a god-send for me; it was mainly because of him that the task of directing a Play with Anant in lead role became manageable.

I was going through the script and the cues; just one day was left for the Play to be staged. I was feeling tired; I thought I could do with a cup of tea.

I walked towards the kitchen to tell Champa to make me some tea.

Champa's giggle was audible from a distance. I also heard a male voice; I thought Champa's husband Raju was with her inside the kitchen. I was amazed to see Panther coming out of kitchen. Something was cooking between Panther and Champa; I made a mental note to tell Anant before the things went out of hand.

I decided to go to Girls' Hostel to pay a visit to Sudha to see how her preparations, for the role of Juliette, were going on. Sudha pleasantly surprised me by memorizing her lines thoroughly.

'How is Romeo shaping up?' She asked.

'We have a rehearsal this evening and you can see for yourself.' I replied.

Sudha had a big laugh when I told her how much effort it took me to dissuade Anant from calling a helicopter from Mumbai; it was Anant's idea that the modern day Romeo should land in the College Campus in a helicopter, and then be escorted to the stage by Panther and his friends. It would have created such a scene in a quiet place like Dharampur. Besides, Romeo in a helicopter would have converted this tragedy in to a farce. Can one imagine Romeo landing in a helicopter near Capulet's orchard?

'Anant has three sets of costumes; he wants to change after every fifteen minutes.' I gave further update to Sudha.

'We cannot break after every fifteen minutes in a forty minutes Play!' Sudha was shocked.

'I will not permit him to do any such thing.' I said.

Our conversation was interrupted by Mala. She was already dressed for the rehearsal. She was looking very attractive in a Bengali Saree and a large Bindi on her forehead.

'Have you seen Anant? He has promised to take me to the canteen for coffee.' Mala said.

This was very annoying. Anant had time to take Mala to canteen but no time for rehearsals.

I could read Anant's mind. He was treating Mala to coffee as he wanted Sudha to feel jealous.

I grew suspicious that Anant may not stop at this. He may do something stupid after the Play to impress Sudha.

I sounded Karan that he had more than prompting at his hand.

- - - - - -

Chapter XIII

On the Play night, the seats of our College Hall were full, and many boys were standing in the sideways and back. In all, five Plays were lined up. Our College was doing two, and the three other Colleges of Dharampur were doing a Play each. There were prizes for the Best Play, the Best Director, the Best Actor, and the Best Actress. The competition would begin at six and be over by ten. Baldev and Mala's Play Devdas was scheduled at number two, and our Play Romeo & Juliet was to be staged in the end at number five.

The Plays staged by other Colleges were no match for our Plays, so the competition boiled down to Devdas and Romeo & Juliet.

Mala looked gorgeous in Bengali attire and make up, but she was not convincing as Paro; her dialogue delivery was flat, and she was not able to come up with proper expressions.

Baldev stole the show as Director and Actor. Emotionally disturbed persons often turn out as good Actors; and for the role of Devdas, Baldev had just to be himself.

Anant managed a so-so performance ably assisted by Karan's prompting.

But the star of the evening was Sudha. She looked exceptionally beautiful as Juliette in the costume arranged by her mother. Her performance matched her looks, and the audience was completely mesmerized.

Sudha's Best Actress award came as no surprise.

About the Best Actor and the Best Director awards, everybody thought Baldev would walk away with the honors; surprisingly, Anant got the Best Actor award and I got the Best Director Award.

Also, our Play was adjudged as the Best Play. I think Sudha's portrayal of Juliette was so good that it turned the opinion of the judges in our favor, and we were able to make a clean sweep.

Sudha was walking back to the Girls' Hostel, when she was stopped on her way by Panther's friends. It was Anant's plan to scare Sudha; he would arrive at the scene after some time and stop the ruffians from harassing her, so as to make an impression on her. But under the euphoria of winning the Best Actor Award, Anant completely forgot about his plan to 'rescue' Sudha.

I had already alerted Karan who intervened just in time to save further embarrassment to Sudha. In any case, the goons had been instructed by Panther not to go beyond a certain limit. Nevertheless, Karan gave them a good thrashing.

- - - - - -

Chapter XIV

Baldev went home dejected. He did not get the awards he deserved. More than that, he missed a golden opportunity to talk to Sudha.

Sudha had won the Best Actress Award. Baldev wanted to congratulate her, but like always he was slow. His reflexes were so torpid that by the time he could put his thoughts into action, Sudha had already gone. To top it, he came to know that Sudha was bothered by ruffians and Karan rescued her. How he wished he were there in place of Karan.

For Baldev, what happened outside never matched his inner world.

His mother threw a plate at him when Baldev reached home. She was annoyed because Baldev came home so late.

She was not bothered about Baldev's participation in extra-curricular activities. She wanted him home in time to attend to domestic chores. His mother had become physically and mentally sick. She was a foul tempered drug addict who abused her son frequently.

Baldev's father Santosh was a poet and scholar who, like many of his contemporaries, had socialist leanings. He was genuinely sympathetic to the cause of the poor and the exploited. Baldev's grandfather was a rich businessman who wanted his son to join his business, and marry a girl from a rich family known to him. But Santosh hated the materialistic world. He turned down the marriage offer and married Asha, an orphan from Anaath Ashram(orphanage). Santosh had met Asha when he was working for an organization that helped homeless women.

Baldev's mother Asha was good looking, but she was completely spoiled because of the lax environment of the Anaath Ashram she was brought up in. Baldev's father could not spot any flaws in her character because he was a sidha-sadha(naïve) romantic person, who thought he was doing a great social service by marrying an orphan.

Santosh's decision to marry an orphan invited his father's wrath who disinherited him.

For a living, Santosh started teaching and joined some NGOs but he was soon disillusioned. He faced disappointment in personal life also, as Asha started showing her true colors within a few years of marriage. Their relations were further strained after Baldev was born, as Asha turned out to be a highly negligent mother.

Then one day Baldev's father Santosh ended his life.

Baldev's grandfather wanted to keep him but his mother Asha fought a legal battle and got her son's custody. Baldev's grandfather agreed to provide the bare minimum financial help. An Aaya was also arranged for Baldev till he was about ten years of age because Asha was not capable of bringing up a child due to her dependence on drugs and alcohol.

Baldev started drinking in school itself, and picked up all possible bad habits; but he was endowed with the intellectual caliber of his father.

That night Baldev was completely exhausted after five hours of Drama Competition. Then, he was hit by the plate thrown at him by his mother. To top it all, he had to sleep without eating a morsel as his mother had not cooked any meals that night.

- - - - - -

Chapter XV

It was the first week of October. I was invited to a symposium on Indian religions in Ambala Town Hall to speak on Ram Charit Manas. Karan was also participating in the function as an orator on teachings of Guru Nanak.

Baldev and Mala had come to cheer us up. Sudha was also there with her parents. It was her first outing after quite some time. The incidents of sector 17 and the Play night of our College had shaken her confidence.

Anant had gone once again to Mumbai to see his parents and Mamaji.

My turn came at number two, after a scholar had spoken about Buddhism.

I began my speech with a prayer for Lord Ganesha and Deity Sarswati. Then, I said the following.

"Ram Charit Manas is a storehouse not only of great religious teachings; it is also one of the best poetry.

The story was narrated by Lord Shiva to Goddess Paravati. It is believed that the story was overheard by Kak-Bhusundi, a swan in Manas Lake, and then it was told by him to Garuda.

Sage Yagyvalka got it from Garuda and passed it on to Sage Bhardwaj who lived in Prayag (Allahabad), and narrated it on several occasions to the devotees visiting Prayag.

According to Ram Charit Manas, there are four types of devotees: Artharthi (who worship God because they are seeking worldly gains), Aart (who worship the God as they want to get out of the dangerous situations by grace of God), Jigyasu (Who are curious), and Gyani (who have the knowledge). But the ideal thing for a devotee is to worship the God without any desire. Then, he can have perpetual bliss like a creature of water that lives in a pond of Amrit (nectar).

One should have enough sense to discern between good and evil. Such sense develops only by reading good books like Holy Scriptures, and by being in company of good people like Saints.

We have to inculcate right values in our children at a very young age so that they develop good habits and keep the right company.

A strong point of Goswami Tulsi Das, the author of Ram Charit Manas, was that in spite of his accomplishments he was very polite and humble. He said if he started narrating his inadequacies, it would take several volumes of books. He also said that he had the advantage of great works of Saints and Scholars before him. He drew an analogy that even the ants can cross a river by climbing over an already constructed bridge.

According to Goswamiji, there is no difference between Nirgun and Sagun. The God can be both Nirgun(invisible) and Sagun(visible). If the God almighty is Nirgun, the love and affection of devotees make him Sagun. Like, there is no difference between water and ice.

Then I narrated the incidents of Narad Muni's curse and How Raja Bhanupratap was doomed.

Finally, I emphasized that the name of Lord Rama is the ultimate fulfillment. I concluded my speech with the following chopai (couplet) of Ram Charit Manas.

'Mangal Bhawan Amangal Hari, Darawahu soo Dashrath Ajir Bihari.' Jay Shree Ram."

(Lord Ram is Abode of all Happiness and Prosperity, and He removes all misery and unhappiness. He who played (as a child) in Dashrath's Courtyard is requested to show mercy on me.)

After two speakers, it was Karan's turn.

Karan spoke about preaching of Guru Nanak and how the Saint travelled more than 80000 miles on foot to spread his message. The following are the most important teachings of Guru Nanak.

"(1) Nam Japo - Recite the name of God.

(2) Kirt Karo -Earn Honestly

(3) Vand Chhakkhao-Share

Guru Nanak said the following about the God.

'Hai Abhi Sach, Hosi Bhi Sach.'

The meaning is that the God has been true since ages, and will be forever true."

- - - - - -

Chapter XVI

Diwali was just two days away. A fete was organized in our College Playground by Students Union.

Mala's stall was very popular because she had the largest number of friends in the College. Besides, she was ably assisted by Neelu and Garima.

Sudha did not set any stall but she came to visit the fete. Anant did not have patience to set up and manage a stall but he wanted to see the fete. I also went with him as I liked the convivial atmosphere associated with such events.

We stopped at Mala's stall and saw that Sudha was also standing there.

Anant kept talking to Mala and deliberately ignored Sudha. In fact he gave the impression that Sudha did not even exist. He dismissed Sudha's greetings with a mere gesture of hands.

Sudha found it very frustrating and moved to Vijay's stall.

Vijay had set up a stall serving delicious Chhole Bhature. The dish was so much in demand that Vijay had to use three gas cylinders.

Baldev came there looking for an opportunity to talk to Sudha. He had had a quarrel with his mother in the morning, and had to go without lunch; he had consumed a quarter of whisky before coming to the fete.

In his inebriated condition, Baldev tried to light a cigarette. Absent-mindedly, he threw a half burnt match stick on one of the cylinders. Suddenly, there was an explosion and Vijay's stall caught fire. Sudha was stuck in fire and cried for help.

Anant and I rushed towards the stall; Karan and others also came for help. We managed to rescue Sudha and Vijay with great difficulty.

Sudha got only minor burns but Vijay was hospitalized for one month. Sudha took leave for one week to rest at her residence in Chandigarh.

Baldev was inconsolable. He could not forgive himself for being so careless as to cause burn injuries to Sudha, his object of love.

If it was not for Mala, Baldev would have died. He consumed a full bottle of phenyl, but Mala managed to take him to hospital where the irritants were taken out of his stomach just in time to save his life.

Baldev's mother did not even come to see him in the Hospital, and Mala had to look after him all the time.

- - - - - -

Chapter XVII

Mala told Sudha that the goons, who chased her in sector 17 and after the Play, were actually sent by Anant so that he could 'rescue' her at the right time. This impressed Sudha a great deal as she thought it was very romantic.

When Anant helped her out of fire in Vijay's stall, Sudha developed strong feelings for Anant.

Anant and I visited Sudha's house at Chandigarh to find out how she was doing. Sudha gave every indication that she had fallen for Anant. She looked lovingly at Anant and found it hard to avert her gaze. She made us stay at her place for a very long time.

Sudha's mother was very affectionate. She got special dishes made for us and asked us to come again.

This change in Sudha's attitude towards Anant amazed me. When Anant was chasing her, she acted so difficult to get; but when Anant started to deliberately ignore her, she was taking so much interest in him.

It made me remember our Drama Teacher who once quoted the Eighteenth Century French Playwright Nicolas Chamfort.

"A woman is like your shadow; follow her, she flies; fly from her, she follows."

May be my friend Anant understood the psychology of women much better than I did. Or was it simply that he did not care whether Sudha would fall in love with him or not. Anant certainly wanted to impress the most beautiful girl of the college, but I was not sure he was ready to make a commitment. On the other hand, Sudha was of very serious disposition. She believed in Saat Janam Ka Sath(Love that lasts seven lifetimes).

- - - - - -

Chapter XVIII

A nant and Sudha started seeing each other regularly.
Mala thought she could make something out of Baldev who, though erratic, was highly talented.

This was a difficult phase of his life for Baldev. His mother's condition was deteriorating; and whenever he saw Sudha with Anant, he felt like ending his life.

Mala's emotional support came as a life line for Baldev.

I was not quite sure how serious Anant was about Sudha, but Mala told me Sudha was very serious about the relationship. Sudha told Mala that she could not live without Anant, and she was under the impression that Anant loved her back as he was using her name as password for his email account and confidential files.

I thought about having a detailed conversation about the matter with Anant, when a crisis cropped up at our Digs.

Panther had been lucky with his betting on cricket matches, and he lured Champa to run away with him. For three days we were without a cook; we had to eat in the Hostel Mess as guests of our friends. On the fourth day, a male cook arrived from Mumbai who would also drive the car because

Raju was too depressed to function after Champa eloped with Panther.

Anant took this incident in his stride, but I felt guilty about not taking any action in time as I had seen Panther fooling with Champa.

I only wished Panther would keep Champa happy and that no harm would come to her. Some people told me they had seen Panther and Champa boarding a train to Mumbai from Ambala.

Raju started drinking heavily and creating scenes. Ultimately, Anant had to dispatch him to Mumbai.

- - - - - -

Our Half Yearly Exams were round the corner. Before that, we had a cricket match lined up. Anant was not bothered much about the Exams, but he was fairly serious about practicing for the cricket match.

Our Play Ground had been renovated thanks to Anant's initiative and persistence. He persuaded College Administration to allocate adequate funds and he personally monitored the renovation works. The entire set up had a new look so much so that it became one of the best College Play Grounds in the State.

Anant also ensured that Verma Sir made proper arrangements for the maintenance of the Play Ground. Anant may not have been interested in studies, but everybody was impressed with his organizing skills and love for Sports.

Chapter XIX

'I have come to watch Anant play.' Sudha said with enthusiasm and devotion of an ardent lover.

She was looking gorgeous in pink salwar suit. She was a natural beauty, and falling in love had made her look all the more beautiful. Whenever someone mentioned Anant's name, Sudha's rosy cheeks turned beetroot.

Mala was standing nearby with Baldev's hand in her hands. She was also looking very beautiful. If Sudha scored a perfect ten, Mala was around nine.

Shweta was also there to cheer Vijay.

The final cricket match of the tournament was being played between Saint John's College and Government College Dharampur. Anant was slated to bat at number four.

Government College batted first and scored 74 runs, setting a target of 75 for Saint John's. The first two wickets of Saint John's fell only at 10 runs, and it was Anant's turn to bat.

Anant scored eleven runs, after which he was injured trying to hit a six; Sudha ran towards him like a cow for her newborn calf.

Doctor examined Anant and said there was nothing to be worried about. He gave him some pain killers. Then, I and Anant went to a nearby clinic for X-Ray. Sudha wanted to accompany us, but Anant stopped her from doing so.

The X-Ray examination ruled out any fracture; we came back to the playground.

Sudha and Mala were waiting for us anxiously. Baldev had already left for his place as his mother was not well, and he was in no mood to see Anant getting all the attention of Sudha.

Karan had come in to bat at number five and Vijay, who had opened the innings, was still batting. They stabilized the innings.

Three more wickets fell and the score reached 71 for five.

Anant went back to the crease at the fall of Vijay's wicket. He did not want to miss the opportunity to hit the winning shot. Karan was still not out at the other end.

Anant made one run and went to the non-striking end. Karan scored two runs and the team scores were level. It was time for the new over and Anant faced the ball.

Anant made a fine square cut; the ball went out of the boundary leading to Saint John's victory by five wickets. Karan was declared man of the match for his unbeaten 30 runs.

We had a big celebration party that night. Saint John's had won the cricket final after four years.

Anant was wearing a very expensive suit, and Sudha was looking stunning in beige dress.

Baldev asked Sudha to dance with him but she refused; she wanted the first dance with Anant.

Baldev tried his luck again, and requested Sudha one more time for a dance.

She refused again, which made Baldev furious.

Baldev was very touchy; he could not handle rejection by a woman.

He was so jealous and frustrated that he started calling names to Anant.

Anant was patient. He ignored Baldev's expletives.

Baldev was in foul mood. He threw a bottle of beer at Anant, but Anant ducked in time to prevent injury.

Baldev drank so much that he passed out; he had to be carried home.

Home was another scene because Baldev's mother had taken sleeping pills; she got wild when we disturbed her at mid night. She created such a ruckus that neighbors woke up, and we had to come back. We could not take Baldev to Digs because Anant's presence would have woken up the sleeping demons in Baldev, and we were not sure how Anant would react to the second dose of pejoratives from Baldev. So we took him to Karan's room in the Hostel.

- - - - - -

Chapter XX

We were going through our Half Yearly Exams. Anant did not study much but he had acquired sufficient patience to sit through the Exams. There were no more incidents of smoking in the Examination Hall or entering into arguments with the Faculty. This was considered a significant improvement as far as Anant was concerned.

I and Karan were standing outside the Examination Hall. This was our third paper out of six; it was supposed to be the easiest as it was about the Modern Indian History.

Mala came to us and started seeking information about 1857 Movement.

We had become used to Mala's foibles. She was in the habit of imbibing information just before entering the Examination Hall. She was so busy with socializing that she found very little time for studies on regular basis.

Sudha, on the other hand, was a very serious student; she spent hours inside her room preparing for the Exams.

After we had satisfied Mala's queries about 1857 Movement, she took me aside and asked me to speak to Anant to make a firm commitment to Sudha.

'Sudha is already dreaming about engagement and wedding. If Anant is serious, Sudha can talk to her parents.' Mala said.

'Give me some time.' I replied.

- - - - - -

During the winter break, I accompanied Anant to his place at Mumbai. I was very impressed with his mother, Lata Aunty; a very affectionate and religious lady. She took us to the Siddhi Vinayak Temple where we paid our respects.

Anant's father, Basant Uncle, appeared to be a very aggressive, no-nonsense type of businessman with very active social life.

But the main influence in Anant's life is his Mamaji.

Mamaji appeared to be a very imposing personality in his early forties. He did not get married and was heavily into impressing people, obliging them and getting work done through them for other people. What he got out of all this for himself? Well, that gave him power with which he controlled lives of so many people.

When we met Mamaji, he was sitting on a sofa wearing a dark brown Kurta Payjama. He had long hair; he was wearing thick glasses. He had airs of someone who was fully in command, had eyes which could see through any façade; and he was in possession of a keen mind which could plan several moves in advance.

He greeted us with a warm smile.

'Come Anant! And this should be your friend Mohan.'

'Hello, Mohan.' Mamaji greeted me.

'Hello, Sir.' I said and followed Anant's gesture in touching Mamaji's feet.

'I understand Mohan is quite an authority on Ram Charit Manas. 'Mamaji said.

'I am simply trying to emulate Dadaji.'I referred to my grandfather.

'I will take you and Anant to Iskon temple tomorrow; Swami Parmanandji is giving a discourse on Bhagwad Geeta.

We left his place after feeding on some highly sumptuous snacks.

- - - - - -

Chapter XXI

I accompanied Anant on a trip to Goa. It was Christmas Time, and the entire place was reflective of the yuletide spirit with chapels decorated to celebrate the birth of Jesus Christ. We visited a number of churches, and saw numerous artworks and sculptures about the life of Christ. The place was full with holidaymakers who were reveling in the festive atmosphere of Christmas Time in Goa.

On our way back to Mumbai, I asked Anant about Sudha.

'She is a nice girl to go around with. I do care for her, but I am not going to marry her.' Anant said.

It was not the right time for Anant to decide about getting married. He was planning to go abroad the next year for the higher studies. Besides, his emotional attachment to Sudha was not serious enough to turn into a firm commitment.

Sudha was under pressure from her parents to finalize her choice from so many proposals for arranged marriage they had received; since she had given her heart to Anant, she was getting desperate as time was running out for her.

As far as Anant was concerned, Sudha was just a friend. He did not realize how badly Sudha would be hurt if he did not make a commitment.

I did not know how to break the truth to Sudha. I did not want her to be hurt.

Conveying message through Mala was also not a good idea.

May be the time will set everything right. C'est la vie.

Chapter XXII

I came across Verma Sir in the front yard. Our Final Exams were just two days away.

'Ask your friend to be very careful; he will be expelled from the College, if he does anything funny.' Verma Sir said.

'There will be no funny business, I assure you Sir.' I replied.

'I hope so!' Verma Sir said.

'Yes Sir! I am positive. Anant is alright Sir. It is just that he is poor in Math, and the paperwork is not his cup of tea.' I tried to defend Anant.

Suddenly Mala appeared from nowhere.

'Give us some tips (guess paper) for the first paper, Sir.' Mala said.

Mala was looking very attractive in a light blue dress.

'I wish I could.' Verma Sir left us with a smiling face. He had to tutor his son Bunty for his fifth standard tests.

We all knew about the College's strict no tips policy. But Mala always tried. If Verma Sir was impervious to her charm, she could always use the second option by buying chocolates and popcorn for Bunty.

I had to dissuade her from doing it. I told her we had no use for tips.

I and Karan were too idealistic to use tips.

Vijay, the book worm, had already crammed the entire course content.

Anant could use tips, but he was totally unconcerned.

Baldev's preparations for the Exam suffered because he was trying to compose a long poem on the emotional trauma of unrequited love.

- - - - - -

It was Saturday when we finished the last question-paper.

We organized a party in the Main Hall.

Sudha herself asked Anant to dance with her, without waiting for him to ask her.

Coming from such a cultured background, Anant could not refuse to dance when asked by a lady; but he danced mechanically without touching her.

Then, Anant invited Mala and Neelu and had a very intimate dance with them. He was giving a clear message to Sudha that he was not a one woman man.

Sudha felt devastated. She felt like leaving immediately, but her feelings for Anant stopped her from doing it. There were rumors that Anant might go to America the next year. She was so much in love with him that she couldn't even think about marrying someone else.

'I want to have a word with you, Anant! Can we go out in fresh air?' She said

'I have nothing to say to you, Madam!' Anant was curt.

There is only so much a girl can put up with; Sudha left the Hall in tears.

I, Karan and Garima followed her.

'Why is this happening to me? My life is completely shattered'. Sudha was crying.

We tried to comfort her but she was inconsolable.

I asked Garima to accompany Sudha to her hostel room.

- - - - - -

Part II

Mumbai - After Five years

Chapter 1

I was going through my papers in my hotel room near Churchgate. I had been invited to give a pravachan on Ram Charit Manas and family values in the Birla Hall. My research team had done a good job, and I had plenty of material at hand.

After my graduation from St John's in Dharampur, I contemplated writing the Civil Services Exam; but my grandfather wanted me to pursue the family profession of katha vachan (reciting scriptures).

The phone rang up. It was Lata Aunty, Anant's mother.

'Mohan, why are you staying in a hotel? 'She said.

'Shift right away to our house.' She spoke further without waiting for my reply.

'Aunty, I will look you up after I am through with my pravachan.' I said.

'Do not be too late! Anant is coming back from USA this evening.' She said.

After Dharampur, Anant went to USA to do a Course in Sports Management.

Sudha was out of Anant's mind; but she waited for him, and she resisted all attempts of her parents to get her engaged.

- - - - - -

The Birla Hall was completely filled with the audience. By this time, I had become quite famous in my field of kathavachan.

I began my speech which was also being covered by Radio and TV.

"There is no granth (scripture) that can match Ram Charit Manas in developing family values. In modern times, when the joint family system is breaking down, Ram Charit Manas shows us the right path.

Ram Charit Manas gives us a strong message of duty, sacrifice and high moral values. Lord Ram was an ideal son. He gracefully accepted Vanvas (exile) so that his father could keep his word. Laxman voluntarily accompanied Ram to Jungle, and Bharat refused to enjoy the perks and privileges of a ruler in Ram's absence.

In our country, parents make so many sacrifices for their children; therefore, it is the duty of the children to take care of their parents in the times of need. The Old Age Homes are not meant for a country like India where the entire fabric of the society is built around selfless love, duty and sacrifice. We should never forget that Joint family and religion are the most important pillars of strength for the emotional health of an individual.

If any of the listeners have broken out of a joint family, they should immediately call their family and say sorry.

I will urge upon all the sons and daughters living abroad to take an oath to talk at least once every week to their parents living in India."

Chapter II

In the evening I went to Anant's palatial house.

Anant had not yet arrived. Lata Aunty was sitting on sofa with an extremely beautiful woman by her side.

'Meet Nalini. She is the new Executive Director. 'Lata Aunty said.

'Basant wants Anant to learn the ropes from her.' She added

Nalini looked too young to be an Executive Director.

Later, I came to know that Nalini was a widow; her husband died in an air crash. She had an adorable daughter, Diya, who was around four years of age. Nalini used to help her husband with business, and she was very good at it because she had done MBA from Australia where she was born and brought up.

Basant Uncle never regretted his decision to appoint Nalini as the Executive Director, because she proved herself to be exceptionally competent.

Lata Aunty admired Nalini and called her Beauty with Brains.

Nalini lived separately in a nearby flat but she and her daughter were frequent visitors to Basant Uncle's house; Young Diya had become darling of the household.

Shortly, Anant arrived from the Airport. He was looking very fit and cheerful. His father's employees welcomed him with flower bouquets; Lata Aunty rushed to give a welcome hug to him.

Anant was so pleased to find me there.

'Hello, Mohan. What a pleasant surprise!'

'Hello, Anant. I missed you so much. 'I said.

'Yes. We have so much to catch up.' Anant said.

Anant had so many queries about Baldev, Karan, Mala, Neelu, and Garima; even Verma Sir! But he did not say a word about Sudha. As far as he was concerned, Sudha was a closed chapter.

I had my dinner at Anant's place, and returned to my hotel.

- - - - - -

Chapter III

The receptionist told me a woman had come to the hotel three times asking for me. She had not given her name and address but she would come again the next morning.

I wondered who the woman might be. Why was she not disclosing her identity?

When I got up the next morning, the room bearer brought a message for me that the same woman was waiting in the lobby wanting to see me.

It was my policy not to see female visitors in my room, so I decided to go to the lobby to see the mysterious woman.

It was Champa who started crying once I went near her. I was too astounded to react.

'My life is ruined, Sahib. Panther brought me to this city and we lived in his friend Razaq's house for about a month. Then, Panther disappeared and Razaq sold me to a brothel.' She managed to speak with great difficulty.

'Somehow I escaped and now I have to work as a part time maid at three places to get two square meals.' She further said.

I did not know what to say.

'I read about you in a newspaper. May be you can help me, Sahib.' She said.

'Why did you not go to Anant Sahib's house?' Finally, I found something to say.

'I am too scared to go there, Sahib.' She replied.

'Is there any news of my husband, Sahib?' She asked me.

All I could recall, Raju was drunk most of the time after Champa eloped with Panther; Anant had to send him back to Mumbai. After sometime, I heard Raju had become an auto rickshaw driver in Delhi.

'You think he will take you back?' I asked.

'I will fall on his feet and apologize; I am a sinner who cannot be forgiven, but I will work as his Dasi (servant).' She said.

'I will find out about Raju.' I said.

Champa left after touching my feet.

I got back to my room and was just about to leave for my pravachan, when the telephone started ringing.

It was Mala. This was a big day for surprises!

'Panditji, I heard you were in Mumbai. I want to invite you to premiere of Baldev's debut film.'

Baldev had brought his mother to Mumbai for treatment of cirrhosis in Jaslok Hospital, and Mala came with him to help them as Baldev was unable to manage anything by himself.

Baldev was emotionally drained out and financially broke. Mala was like manna in desert for him. She got a job as a receptionist in a hotel, and rented a small flat.

Baldev showed no inclination to work. In any case, he could not do anything other than writing or directing Plays. Mala contacted Anant who was in USA and sought appointment with Anant's Mamaji.

With Mamaji's blessings, Baldev got a job as an Assistant Director in a film. Since he was cut out for this kind of task, his work was appreciated and he got two more films as Assistant Director.

Finally, Baldev got a chance to work as a full-fledged Director when Mamaji managed finances for a movie Baldev wanted to direct. The movie 'Bandhan' was to be premiered on Friday in Roxy cinema.

'He has changed! He drinks only on social occasions.' Mala said.

'You are a positive influence in his life.' I praised Mala.

'How is his Mother?' I asked.

'There is some improvement, but she is in and out of hospital frequently.' Mala replied.

'Where is Baldev? 'I asked.

'He has gone out for promotion of the movie. I will send the invite to your hotel. See you on Friday.'

Mala hung up.

- - - - - -

Chapter IV

Anant's parents were waiting for him for breakfast; Anant was late as he was trying to sleep off his jetlag.

Nalini and Diya were invited for breakfast. Nalini was looking very beautiful in almond color dress. Young Diya was looking like a doll.

'Good morning Nalini.' Basant said.

'Good morning Sir.' Nalini replied.

'Good morning.' Young Diya echoed. Everybody at the table responded enthusiastically.

After some time, Anant came downstairs and took his seat.

Nalini threw a big smile at Anant who nodded politely.

Lata introduced Nalini to Anant.

'Nalini is our new Executive Director. You will work with her for two months to learn about our business.' Lata said.

'What is the hurry? Ma! Give me a break!' Anant said.

They started eating quietly.

Basant and Lata were having paranthas.

Anant was having french toast and beans.

Nalini lived in style twenty four into seven; for the breakfast, she was having quarter boiled eggs and cabbage salad.

Sometime in the middle of the breakfast, Diya lost her balance and fell off the chair. She was crying as she injured her fore head on which there was a slight bruise.

Anant left his breakfast half way, and held Diya in his arms. One of the domestic helps brought the first aid kit. Anant applied anti septic to Diya's injury.

He was surprised at his own response; he did not know he had such a strong maternal instinct. He asked the help to call Dr Desai, their family doctor.

Dr Desai came within ten minutes; he applied a small bandage, and gave a tetanus shot to Diya.

'I am floored, Anant!' Nalini was at her charming best.

'You really love children!' She continued.

'Oh, it is nothing.' Anant said.

- - - - - -

Chapter V

Anant got busy with his social life. Almost every day, he went out partying with his friends and came back home after mid night.

After one such party, he came home around two o' clock. His mother was still awake.

'Are you alright? Ma!' Anant asked.

'I have a slight headache.' Lata replied. She was a patient of chronic hypertension.

Anant's father Basant had gone on a business trip to Singapore.

Nalini was spending the night with her sister in Pune. She had left Diya in Lata's care.

Anant took out a tablet of crocin from the medicine cabinet and gave it to Lata.

Diya's Aya Gulabi came out of the guest room.

'Baby is running fever.' She said.

Anant went with her to the guestroom, and touched Diya's fore head. It felt warm.

Anant spoke to Dr Desai over phone.

Doctor Desai suggested Diya be given half a tablet of crocin. He said he would examine her first thing in the morning, and he may have to run some tests.

Anant gave Diya the medicine and also applied cold sponge. The fever came down but Anant could not sleep. He was awake the whole night nursing Diya; even though Diya's Aaya Gulabi and four domestic helps of his own house were there to perform the task.

Nalini returned the next day; she could not thank Anant enough.

Lata was pleasantly surprised to discover this part of Anant's personality. She had the impression that Anant cared only about his pleasures.

She thought it was time Anant got settled. Her friend's daughter Smita would be the right choice as her bahu (daughter in law). She had already made a commitment of sorts to Smita's mother.

- - - - - -

Chapter VI

Roxy cinema was house full on premiere of 'Bandhan'. Many big shots of the Movie World attended the premiere. The response of the audience was highly encouraging.'

'Bandhan' was an emotional drama about a troubled man-woman relationship, and Baldev's direction was superb.

I saw Baldev after five years; he was looking a mature adult with beard and glasses.

'Congratulations, Baldev!' I said.

'Oh! Hello, Mohan! It has been such a long time.' Baldev said.

'Yes, I am so pleased to see you. This movie of yours is going to be a big success.'

'I need best wishes of my friends, particularly yours.'

We were joined by Mala who was looking very attractive in mauve sleeveless blouse and saree.

'It was so nice of you, Mohan, to find time to come here!' She said.

Baldev was soon cornered by the reporters.

'He has made it, Mala.' I said.

'Yes, He worked so hard.' She responded

'You are his muse.' I said.

'I have hardly done anything.' was Mala's reply.

'You are everything to him.' I said.

I was amazed at how much a woman can transform a man. Baldev had metamorphosed from a feckless alcoholic to a confident Movie Director.

'There is another surprise for you, Mohan!' Mala said.

I followed Mala to the opposite side of the lobby.

I spotted Sudha who was looking very beautiful in a chestnut color salwar suit. She had flown from Guwahati to Mumbai on Mala's invitation to be at the premiere. Those present in the lobby gave her admiring looks. She could have been mistaken for an aspiring actress.

Sudha's father was transferred from Chandigarh to Guwahati. She completed her graduation from Cotton College Guwahati.

Sudha resisted every attempt of her parents to get her married. She was still pining for Anant. In fact, her main motive behind coming to Mumbai was to have an interaction with Anant.

Mala had also invited Anant, but he sent a last minute apology with a bouquet of flowers offering his best wishes for success of Baldev's movie.

'Hello, Sudha. I am so pleased to see you! How have you been?' I said.

'Hello, Mohan.' Sudha said with a smile.

Three of us were silent for some time.

'Why don't you visit Assam? It is such a beautiful place.' Sudha said.

'I have plans to visit Tezpur. Karan has invited me.' I said.

Our friend Karan had joined Indian Revenue Service and was posted as Assistant Commissioner Income Tax in Tezpur.

'Karan has never met me, though I get cards from him on New Year and my birthday' Sudha said.

'He must be busy.' I said.

'Let us surprise him! Four of us should visit his place. I want Baldev to get a break from this mad business of movie making.' Mala said.

'Do you remember Vijay, the book worm?' Sudha asked.

'Yes, of Course I do.' I said.

'He has joined ONGC(Oil and Natural Gas Commission) as a geologist. I met him when he was working in Jorhat. Then, he was transferred to Barmer.' Sudha informed.

I said bye to Sudha and Mala as I was getting late for my pravachan.

- - - - - -

Chapter VII

Anant's family owned a large Guest House in Mahabaleswar. The family had come there for a relaxed weekend. Nalini and Diya were also with them.

They were having lunch after a leisurely Saturday morning of golf and swimming.

Little Diya insisted on having Achar (pickles). Anant fed her a liberal spoonful.

'So much Achar is not good for her.' Lata said.

'How is Anant concerned? I will have to put up with Diya's indigestion'. Nalini said.

The reason for Nalini's outburst was that she was peeved with Anant as he had refused to take her out to dinner.

Nalini had become very fond of Anant.

'If someone likes a child so much, he has to be a very good human being'. She once told a friend of hers.

Nalini was an extremely beautiful woman and very proud. She was a widow but she was still highly sought after. She was not yet past twenty five, and many men craved for her attentions.

Anant was impressed with Nalini, but he did not have any special feelings for her. He saw her mainly as Company's

Executive Director and Diya's mother, and treated her with respect.

As time passed, Nalini was developing feelings for Anant. Gradually, her fondness for Anant was turning into emotional attachment.

Nalini was baffled. She was getting strangely drawn towards Anant. Was it only because he was so attached to Diya? Or, was it the charm of Anant's personality? Anant was so young, fresh and energetic. The other day when she joined Anant in playing 'hide and seek' with Diya, she felt so good she wished it to last forever.

It was not a simple attraction towards the opposite sex. Nor was it that in Anant she saw security of marriage and a father for Diya. It was more than that.

She planned to spend some time alone with Anant to sort out her feelings.

'I am getting very bored. Why don't we go some place for dinner?' She asked Anant one evening.

It was very difficult to resist Nalini's charm, but somehow Anant was not prepared to date her.

When he refused, Nalini was upset; and since her emotions were very transparent, everybody noticed a peculiar kind of tension between her and Anant.

Smita came to stay with them in Mahabaleswar Guest House for Saturday evening.

Nalini felt strong pangs of jealousy. Was it because Lata had almost finalized Smita as her future daughter in law?

Nalini wondered why she was in the grip of such feelings. But she kept her cool.

After breakfast, all of them went for boating. Nalini did not exchange a single word with Anant, and she was barely polite with others.

Smita left after lunch.

In the afternoon, Diya was playing in the lobby and Anant picked her up fondly.

'Do not touch my baby! Stay away from her!' Nalini blasted.

Anant was nonplussed. He was offended by Nalini's behavior but did not know how to react. He went quietly to his room.

- - - - - -

Chapter VIII

It was around midnight and Anant was in deep slumber in his room in the Guest House. Suddenly, he felt a gentle touch on his face and a strong fragrance of Dolce and Gabbana perfume filled his nostrils. He woke up to see Nalini sitting on the edge of his bed. She was wearing a pink negligee with her luxuriant hair spread over her shoulders.

'I am terribly sorry, Anant. I snapped at you. I do not know what became of me! 'She said and started sobbing.

'Oh, it is alright.' Anant said consoling her.

After a while, Nalini regained her composure.

'Do you have feelings for me?' She asked looking into Anant's eyes.

Anant did not say anything. He was in the grip of feelings he had never experienced before.

- - - - - -

Next day, Anant came to see me in Pune, where I was on a pravachan tour.

'I am going to marry Nalini.' He said.

'What about Sudha?' I remarked. I also told him that Sudha had come to Mumbai for Bandhan's premiere hoping to meet him.

'Nalini is the one for me.' He said.

Anant's mind was made up. Man woman relationships are highly complex. Quite often, lifelong decisions are made on spur of the moment.

It is difficult to say why Anant preferred Nalini to Sudha; I think it was Anant's affection for Diya that ultimately turned the scales. But Anant had practically ruined Sudha's life though he had no intention of doing so.

I had mixed feelings.

Though I felt extremely sorry for Sudha, I was relieved that Anant was settling into domesticity, and he would begin a new chapter in life.

There was an additional bit of good news: I got a call from Mala telling me that she and Baldev were getting married.

On the next Ram-Navami Anant got married to Nalini, and Baldev got married to Mala.

The same day, Sudha took an overdose of sleeping pills. Doctors saved her life but she had to be in the hospital for almost a month, and developed long term health problems.

Her parents arranged a marriage proposal for her. She was too weak and broken to resist.

Next June, she was married to Mr. Sikri, who had just come back from abroad after doing MBA.

- - - - - -

Part III

Ramnagar
and Mumbai -
After Five More Years

Chapter 1

Ramnagar was an industrial township, in Central India, where manufacturers lined up to set up Steel Plants mainly because of availability of iron ore and cheap labor. The place was also known for its love for Sports as it had four big Sports Stadia and it could boast of having hosted all major Sports tournaments.

Anant's family possessed a huge Steel Plant called Basant Steel in Ramnagar. Anant was made in charge of the Steel Plant after his marriage so that he could head an independent enterprise.

Apart from running the Steel Plant, Anant also took active interest in Sports. The family's business rival, Rajshree Steel, not only had higher Steel production; they also controlled the Sports Stadia and selection of teams.

It was 10th wedding anniversary of Kamal, the CMD of Rajshree Steel; a gala party was arranged in hotel Gaylord, and all the big shots of Ramnagar were invited to the party.

Anant and Nalini arrived late. It was a status symbol to come late. Besides, Nalini took a lot of time in getting ready. Though she was a natural beauty, Nalini always took care that her make-up was perfect.

Nalini's entry in a party was always the highlight of the evening. She was easily the most beautiful woman around. She was very charming too.

The hosts, Kamal and his wife Kanta, greeted them warmly.

Nalini was soon surrounded by admirers. She loved socializing; Anant was slightly reserved.

Anant was standing near the bar with a glass of whiskey in his hand when Posco, a local businessman and former sportsman, came to him.

'How are you Anant?' Posco said.

'I am fine' Anant said.

'How is the business?' Posco asked.

'A bit slow.' Anant remarked.

'Are you coming to see tomorrow's match?' Posco wanted to know.

'No! Not in that shithouse.' Anant was referring to the Central Stadium where the big match was to be played.

Anant was not happy with the way Kamal and company maintained the playgrounds. He could have done a much better job given his Sports Education in USA. But he was helpless because Rajshree Steel had control over seven of the eleven members of the Committee that had the management of everything to do with Sports in Ramnagar.

'I know what you mean'. Posco said.

'I can swing two Committee Members against Rajshree.' Posco further said.

'How?' Anant asked.

'They have some business interests in Mumbai. The new DCP is after their blood. If your Mamaji puts in a word to the powers that be, they can live peacefully.' Posco said.

'Why would Mamaji do such a thing?' Anant said.

'He can't say no to his favorite nephew. If you are in charge of the Sports Stadia and the teams, it can give a new life to Sports. Former players like me have been waiting for such a long time for someone like you who can put things in order.' Posco said.

'I will think about it'. Anant ended the conversation.

- - - - - -

Chapter II

The next day at breakfast, Anant told Nalini about his conversation with Posco.

'I think you should speak with Mamaji'. Nalini said.

She very much liked the idea of Anant getting actively involved in Sports Administration.

Being Anant's wife, she knew what was after his heart.

'But Mamaji would not like to do it'. Anant said.

'Why not? It is a very small favor!' Nalini said.

'I would rather not talk to Mamaji about this'. Anant was facing a dilemma. He disliked such maneuvers, but it was the sine qua non for doing anything worthwhile in Sports.

'You must do it in the interest of Sports.' Nalini said getting up. She had to go to Diya's school for the Parent Teachers Meet.

Nalini knew it would be embarrassing for Anant to request Mamaji; so that evening she rang up Basant, and requested him to speak to his brother in law.

In the next meeting of the Committee, Basant Steel wrested control of Sports from Rajshree Steel.

Kamal took it sportingly and assured Anant of his full co-operation.

'Well done Anant!' Mamaji was ebullient.

'I have hardly done anything.' Anant was being modest. He was in Mumbai paying his customary visit to Mamaji.

'In a short period of six months, you have completely transformed the playgrounds from district level to the world class.' Mamaji said.

'Have you gone through the concept paper I mailed you?'Anant asked.

'Yes, I have. It is a million dollar idea! I appreciate your vision about improvement in Sports facilities for young aspirants throughout the country.' Mamaji said.

'That is my dream!' Anant said.

'Why don't you take Lata with you to Ramnagar? She can do with some fresh air.' Mamaji changed the topic.

'Hmm!' was all that Anant could say.

His mother Lata was just out of hospital. Her constant high blood pressure had damaged her kidneys. But taking her to Ramnagar was not such a good idea; Lata and Nalini were not on the best of terms.

Lata did not like Anant's decision to marry Nalini. She had to go back on her promise to Smita's mother, and she did not like the way Nalini dominated Anant. Soon, Nalini and Lata were not on friendly terms.

- - - - - -

Chapter III

I got two invitations: the first one was for a pravachan in Ramnagar, and the second one for Ram Katha in Barmer; only one day separated the two invitations. The two places were not only located in two different States; they were more than 1500 km apart. Nevertheless, I accepted both the invitations because I would be able to meet Anant in Ramnagar and Vijay in Barmer.

In Ramnagar, My pravachan was in Ramlila Ground where thousands of devotees gathered to hear my speech on what Lord Ram said to the residents of Ajodhya after returning from Vanvas. I referred to the following.

"Sunhu Sakal Purjan Mam Vani'(Please listen to me my countrymen) Lord Ram spoke to his subjects.

It is very fortunate that one is born as a human being. This privilege is not available even to devtas (gods). I quoted the following chopai of Ram Charit Manas.

'Bade Bhag Manus Tan Pawa. Sur Durlabh Sab Granth Hi Gawa.'

Those who indulge in vices and luxuries, waste this great opportunity. In fact they convert nectar to poison, and exchange philosopher's stone (paras mani) for marble.

'Gunja Grahai, Parasmani Khoi'

The path of bhakti (devotion) leads to every happiness, but bhakti cannot be attained without association with Saints (Satsang).

The ideal citizen is one who bears no ill will, does not enter into any conflict; has no desire, or fear.

I made the following quote.

'Bair Na Vigrah, Aas Na Trasha. Sukhmaya Tahi Sada Sab Masa.'

Lord Ram also asked his countrymen to be just and fair. Everybody should be treated equally, and there should be the rule of dharma.

Another important message from Ram Charit Manas is that for an individual welfare of others should come before any other consideration, and there is no sin bigger than hurting others. I quoted the following chopai of Ram Charit Manas.

"Parhit Saras Dharam Nahi Bhai. Par Pida Sum Nahi Adhmai."

Following the practice of my grandfather, I suggested that everybody should recite Sundarkand during Navratra, and each family should donate one rupee per family member per day to a Goshala.

- - - - - -

Chapter IV

When I came back from my pravachan, little Diya was back from school. She was looking like a young princess. Absolutely adorable!

I was so happy to see the domestic bliss of my friend Anant.

Anant came back from office. He was on top of the world. His company had made record profits. He would also be able to garner adequate funds to implement his vision. Soon, he would transform the Sports Scenario.

'I am throwing a party tonight; there is a big surprise coming your way!' Anant said.

'Tell me what it is.' I said.

'Wait till the evening.' Anant said.

To celebrate his success, Anant threw a big party that evening in Gaylord Hotel. All important people from Ramnagar were there. Important Sports Personalities and Big Business Tycoons from Delhi, Mumbai, Kolkata, and Chennai were also present in the party.

Around nine thirty, the entry of three guests pleasantly surprised me. Baldev and Mala entered with a stunningly beautiful girl in her early twenties.

Baldev was shooting in Ramnagar for his new film 'Aaina'; the strikingly beautiful girl accompanying Baldev and Mala was Sayeeda, the debutant heroine of 'Aaina'.

Before Sayeeda's entry, the host Nalini was the main attraction. Then, the focus shifted to Sayeeda as everybody wanted her attention. The hotel management had to organize extra security as many persons wanted to enter Gaylord hotel to catch a glimpse of Sayeeda.

With guests piling on to Sayeeda, it became easier for me to have conversation with Baldev and Mala.

Baldev had given three more hits after 'Bandhan' and was now ranked among the top Movie Directors. He had bought a posh bungalow in Irish Park, Juhu.

In his forthcoming movie 'Aaina' Baldev was introducing a new heroine.

Mala was looking slightly plump; actually, she was expecting. I blessed her and wished she should have a very healthy child.

Baldev was soon surrounded by sycophants. The guests at Anant's party worshipped success.

I withdrew to a quiet corner with a glass of orange juice in my hand.

Next morning at the Airport, I had another surprise. I was waiting for the boarding call of my Mumbai flight when I saw a familiar female face from some distance. I got up and walked to her; it was Sudha.

She was still very beautiful, but she was looking pale and emaciated; there were dark circles under her eyes.

'Hello, Sudha.' I said.

'Oh, Hello, Mohan! Fancy seeing you here!' She said.

'Where are you off to?' I asked.

'I am going to Hyderabad to attend my cousin's wedding.' She said.

'I moved to Ramnagar only a month ago. My husband Mr. Sikri is Chief General Manager of Rajshree Steel.' She added.

'I came here for a pravachan.' I said.

'I know. I read in the papers.' She said.

I decided against mentioning Anant and his family to Sudha. I thought she might get upset.

'Did you see Anant?' She herself brought it up.

A look at Sudha's face was enough to tell that she was still in love with Anant.

'Yes. In fact, I stayed at his place.' I said.

'Why did he marry that woman?' There was more concern in her voice than query.

'I do not know. Anant was always unpredictable. But he is a changed man now.' I said.

'Changed man, my foot! He still remains a confused loser. He wants to help people but ends up hurting them.' Sudha exploded.

'Some people are simply exploiting his energy and enthusiasm. He will regret one day that he let himself be used by heartless and ruthless people.' She added.

Maybe this was a hurt woman speaking. But no one can paint a truer picture of a man than the woman who is in love with him.

My flight was announced. I had to say bye to Sudha.

I came from Ramnagar to Mumbai where a chartered plane awaited me. The organizers of Ram Katha at Barmer had made the arrangements for my travel and stay.

- - - - - -

Chapter V

After Ram Katha in Barmer, I met Vijay who was now working in a senior position in ONGC. His wife Shweta was working in Oil India Limited in Jaisalmer.

Vijay had worked very hard for oil and gas exploration in Barmer and Jaisalmer districts. But his efforts were not rewarded with success. On several occasions, his team came very close to striking oil but they met with disappointment.

'It is so frustrating. I do not know what to do?' Vijay said.

'For the last five years, I have worked twenty hours a day but to no avail. I am exasperated.' He continued.

'Are you sure there is oil in Barmer?' I asked.

'ONGC teams have been exploring for the last fifty years. Now they have a joint venture with a Multinational Company. I am very sanguine on the basis of the work done so far.' Vijay said.

'The thing is, we are not able to hit the precise location.' He added.

'I wish you all the luck. You should follow your passion, and keep your nose to the grindstone.' I gave him a pep talk.

Shweta's office was near Indo-Pak Border where Oil India teams were working on gas exploration. I and Vijay went there in the evening.

We went to see the Border with Shweta. On our way back to Shweta's office, we stopped at Tanot Mata Temple which is a very important Shakti Peeth (divine seat of power) of the deity Aavad. This temple has been associated with a number of miracles. Since it is so close to the Border, it is maintained by BSF.

I insisted on going inside the temple.

Vijay had to come with me because I was his guest. Otherwise, he did not believe in temples.

The Priest worshipped Tanot Mata.

"Ya Devi Sarva Bhuteshu, Shakti Rupen Samsthita, Namo Tasyai, Namo Tasyai, Namo Tasyai, Namo Namah."

(Salutation to the Goddess who is present as a divine force in all Beings)

The BSF Pujari (Priest) gave 'Prasad' to me, Vijay and Shweta.

Sometime in the following week in Delhi, I read in the papers that oil had been struck in Barmer.

I was reminded of the following quote by Ben Carson.

"Through hard work, perseverance and a faith in God, you can live your dream."

- - - - - -

Chapter VI

Sayeeda was born in a middle class family in Moradabad. Her father was a shopkeeper with modest means, but he spent a substantial amount of money on Sayeeda's education.

Sayeeda completed her graduation from a prestigious College, and learned music and dance.

Sayeeda inherited her good looks from her mother, Nazneen, who was very conservative. Nazneen wanted to marry off Sayeeda the moment she was out of the College. But Sayeeda had ambitions; she did not want to waste her looks and talents by becoming a housewife so early.

Sayeeda's Phupha (husband of father's sister), Abdul, lived in Mumbai; he earned his living by supplying decoration material for film sets.

He had contacts with a number of film wallahs (persons). During Baldev's Assistant Director days, Abdul did regular business with him.

Sayeeda was getting sick of her mother's pressure to consider the marriage proposals.

With her indulgent father's permission, Sayeeda visited her Buwa (Father's sister) and Phupha in Mumbai, and shared with them her ambition to be a model or a film actor.

Abdul knew Baldev, but by that time Baldev had become an established Movie Director.

It took almost two months of regular visits to studios for Abdul to arrange Sayeeda's meeting with Baldev, but it was worth the effort.

Baldev saw in Sayeeda what he was searching for a very long time. She would be perfect for heroine's role in 'Aaina'. Sayeeda was very beautiful and charming, had lots of sex appeal and very expressive eyes; she also had perfect Urdu diction which is so difficult to find in modern day heroines.

His mind was made up to cast Sayeeda as heroine of 'Aaina' but the producer wanted an established one, because it was a big budget movie.

The only way out was to use good offices of Mamaji. One call from Mamaji would be enough for the producer to agree to Baldev's choice.

He asked Mala to convince Mamaji. After all it was Mala who, during his initial lean phase, got an appointment with Mamaji through Anant; and Mamaji helped them at every stage.

This time Mala was reluctant. She did not like the idea of seeking favors from Mamaji only so that Sayeeda could be launched. She did not see anything special in Sayeeda. Any other heroine could have done just as well.

Baldev was adamant. No Sayeeda, no Movie! For the first time after their wedding, Baldev and Mala had a huge fight.

Ultimately Mala gave in; she had already done so much for Baldev. How could she disappoint him?

The more we are invested in a relationship, the more are we likely to be emotionally exploited into doing irrational things.

Mala made a phone call to Mamaji.

- - - - - -

Baldev, Mala and Sayeeda were sitting in the drawing room waiting for Mamaji.

Mala was not liking it. The presence of nubile Sayeeda was giving her a complex.

Mamaji came to the drawing room after they had waited for more than an hour.

Baldev and Mala touched Mamaji's feet.

Sayeeda folded her hands and said Namaste.

'So! This is your new heroine.' Mamaji said.

'Yes Sir. She wants your blessings.' Baldev said.

'She is a Makhan Bada(Candy)!'Mamaji said.

They were all surprised at the language Mamaji used. Sometimes, even the best of men make social gaffes when in presence of an exceptionally beautiful woman.

Mamaji's mobile rang up. He went into an inner room to take the call.

His loud voice was partly audible in the drawing room. He was giving a piece of his mind to some politician.

He came back to the drawing room.

'I will see what I can do.' He said and the meeting was over.

Next day, Baldev got a call from his producer. Sayeeda was in.

- - - - - -

Chapter VII

It was Diwali and Lata was feeling low. She missed Anant. She also missed Nalini, who as a daughter-in-law symbolized the Goddess Laxmi; since Nalini's marriage with Anant, the family businesses were doing exceptionally well.

She performed special puja in Siddhi Vinayak and Maha Laxmi Temples. Thereafter, she lit 108 lamps and distributed sweets and clothes to the poor.

She was a pious, religious lady; a devoted wife and a caring mother; but she had health issues. She found it difficult to keep her blood pressure under control. It had started affecting her kidneys. She had already been hospitalized twice because of high creatinine levels. She was feeling physically and emotionally worn out.

Basant was busy playing cards with his friends. It was his habit to play cards on Diwali night, and usually he and his friends got so involved that they played till the small hours of the morning.

Lata felt lonely and depressed; all her money and domestic helps could not bring her any cheer.

Anant and Nalini had visited her only once after their marriage. Anant's decision to marry Nalini, instead of his mother's choice Smita, created tension in the family.

Nalini knew Lata wanted Anant to marry Smita and would never have accepted Nalini as her bahu if she could have her way with Anant's decision. This made her feel embarrassed; with time, there developed a communication gap between Nalini and Lata. Eventually, they stopped talking to each other.

Maybe it was her fault, Lata thought. She should have respected Anant's decision to marry Nalini, and she should not have made a commitment to Smita's mother without consulting Anant.

Lata phoned her brother and wished him happy Diwali.

'Happy Diwali, Lata.' Mamaji's voice boomed over phone.

'If you speak with Anant, please ask him to visit us for the Christmas and New Year. We may plan a visit to Goa.' Lata told her brother.

'Sure! Goodnight, Lata.' Mamaji disconnected.

- - - - - -

Chapter VIII

Kamal of Rajshree Steel did not mind losing control of the Sports Committee. In fact he was secretly relieved to be away from the tensions associated with the big matches. But his new Chief General Manager Sikri was very ambitious and crafty.

'Sir, we should buy a team.' He suggested to Kamal.

'I do not want any jhanjhat (tension) of team-sheams.' Kamal said.

'A high profile organization like ours cannot stay out of action Sir.' Sikri said.

'Well! You buy a team. We will help you, Sikri.' Kamal said.

That was all that Sikri needed. With Rajshree money at stake, he would be able to have a risk free shot at making big money. He hated working as an employee of Sethjis; he wanted to have his own business.

The only thing that was needed now was to influence Anant.

Sikri knew that Anant was a big snob and would not like to deal with him directly. After all, a Chief General Manager was just a glorified Munim.

Sikri also knew that Sudha was in College with Anant, and she could be used as a connection to further his interests; but he had to be subtle about it.

Sikri's mind was very fertile. He persuaded Kamal to invite Anant and Nalini for a weekend at Kamal's Farm House. He and Sudha would also be there as Kamal's invitees.

- - - - - -

Around 5pm on Saturday evening, Kamal and Kanta received Anant, Nalini and Diya at Kamal's Farm House about 30 km away from Ramnagar. Sikri was also in attendance.

Sudha pretended a headache and rested in one of the guest rooms. She had to mentally prepare herself for the moment she would face Anant.

Anant, Nalini and Diya went to their room to freshen up.

Around 8pm, they all assembled in the Lawns in front of the Guest House.

Anant was highly surprised when Sudha joined the party. She was looking beautiful in light blue-green saree, though she seemed to have lost weight since Dharampur days.

'This is Mrs. Sikri.' Kamal introduced her.

Oh! Hello, Sudha! Anant said.

'We studied together in St. John's, Dharampur.' He added.

Sikri was smiling. The introduction of his wife had suddenly increased his value in the eye of his employer as well as Anant.

'This is my wife Nalini. Our daughter Diya went to bed early.' Anant said.

Sudha and Nalini said hello to each other.

Though Kanta was a beautiful woman in her own right, she paled in comparison to Sudha and Nalini.

Sudha and Nalini were like two finalists of a beauty contest. If one was compelled to decide in favor of one, the honors would go to Nalini because she exuded more charm and energy. But Sudha was younger, and Anant's presence had brought back roses to her cheeks.

Sudha was very pleased to be in Anant's company. Her marriage with Sikri was loveless. She was extremely happy that the destiny gave her a chance to share a pleasant evening with Anant, even though it was in a group.

Anant was unaffected; he was not much for revisiting the forgotten chapters.

Anant was Romeo only in the Play staged by us in the College, but Sudha followed Juliette's script throughout her life by having undying love for Anant.

Kamal had called the best folk artists in the State who rendered a splendid performance. They all enjoyed a lovely evening of music and dance; which was followed by delicious dinner prepared by Sugan Chand, Kamal's special chef.

The problem with VIPs is that they eat very little. Too much food was left over, which was consumed by Sugan Chand and his helpers.

Sugan Chand, who was in his fifties, could not handle so much rich food and fell ill. So there was a practical problem in the morning about who will prepare the breakfast.

Kanta was still sleeping; Nalini and Sudha went to the kitchen to prepare breakfast.

Nalini's culinary skills were limited, but Sudha was an accomplished cook; besides, Sudha was highly motivated that Anant would eat the food cooked by her.

Breakfast was laid on table by the helpers. To everybody's surprise, Anant didn't touch any dish. He said he was not well and refused to eat at all. Kamal, Kanta, and Nalini urged Anant to eat something as it would not be good to travel on an empty stomach.

For a moment Anant thought that he should be polite and eat at least a little bit, but he couldn't. May be his subconscious mind told him that Nalini would not like him eating and praising Sudha's dishes.

On many occasions, Anant himself could not understand his own complex thought process.

Sudha was devastated. She felt terribly hurt, and excused herself saying her headache was bothering her once again. She went to her room and started crying.

Sikri watched the proceedings with a lot of interest.

- - - - - -

Chapter IX

It was my next trip to Mumbai when I got a call from Mala. She was crying and wanted to see me.

'Why don't you and Baldev come over to my hotel tomorrow for breakfast?' I said.

'I have to see you alone.' Mala said.

'Ok. See you tomorrow.' I said.

Next morning, I was shocked to hear what Mala said.

Baldev had bought a flat in Andheri for Sayeeda, and he was spending most of his evenings with her.

After Aaina's commercial success, Sayeeda was getting many offers. Baldev decided which movie she could accept, and in most of the movies he was the director; but with time, his interest in Sayeeda changed from purely professional to emotional and physical.

Mala was in tears when she told me how Baldev completely ignored her, and she feared he may leave her for Sayeeda. She felt so lonely and lost.

I had read and heard so much about human weakness but this was the limit. In spite of all his talents, Baldev was so ungrateful and depraved. The transient charm of Sayeeda made him forget Mala, the goddess who had taken him out of gutter and nurtured him to be one of the most successful Movie Directors.

I tried to speak to Baldev, but he did not take my call.

After a few days, I learnt that Mala had moved out of Baldev's Irish Park House; she was now living in a small flat in Versova with Baldev's mother, who had recovered from her liver disorder.

Mala delivered a healthy baby boy, who was named Santosh Junior after his grandfather.

Baldev did not even come to see his child.

- - - - - -

Chapter X

Bunty Verma quietly entered the corner room in Hotel Darpan. He was holding a bag full of currency notes.

His friend Ramesh was already there with a seedy looking guy wearing black leather jacket and dark goggles.

'How much have you brought?' Ramesh asked

'Three lac.' Bunty replied.

'Good. You will get nine if your team wins.' Ramesh said taking the bag full of money from Bunty.

Bunty was studying in Saint John's College Dharampur. His father Verma Sir, who retired some time back, was now living in a small house in Kasauli.

Bunty was an average student, but he had all Sports Statistics at his fingertips. He was very fond of watching Sports Channels.

Unfortunately, he fell in bad company, and developed addiction for betting. His childhood friend, Ramesh, had introduced him to the local bookie.

Initially, he had the beginner's luck; he also had the ability to assess the forms of teams and players which helped him make some money.

Then he started betting very high stakes. In the last match, he staked a huge amount on a strong team which was almost certain to win. Quite unexpectedly, some of the players performed so badly that his team lost, and Bunty came under heavy debt. He owed two lac rupees to the local bookie.

The only way to square off the debt was to bet on the final match. This time Ramesh and the bookie insisted on hard cash before the match.

Verma Sir had suffered from frequent attacks of chest pain in the last month. The doctors advised by-pass surgery of the coronary arteries.

Verma Sir withdrew three lac rupees from the bank. He was to go to Chandigarh with his wife the next day for his surgery.

Bunty ran away with the cash which was meant for his father's surgery. With his knowledge of match statistics and form of teams and players, he was confident that he was backing the right team; he thought it was only a matter of time before he would pay off the bookie's debt, and have enough money for his father's operation.

What Bunty did not know was that all the knowledge of statistics and form of teams and players was of no use if the matches were fixed.

- - - - - -

Chapter XI

Posco was having drinks with two gentlemen in his drawing room.

One of them was Mr. Sikri.

The other one could hardly be called a gentleman; he was wearing a red check shirt with green trousers, and there were two big scar marks on his face. He gulped his drink in one shot.

'How was your flight? Panther.' Posco asked.

'It was very comfortable.' Panther said.

Posco refilled Panther's glass.

Panther quaffed his drink.

Sikri was sipping his drink quietly.

When he was an active player, Posco came in contact with some bookies; one of them introduced him to Panther, a close associate of Razaq who was controlling betting operations in five States with the help of his underworld connections.

'If you want to make big money, we have to get details of the team strategy so that we can set the bets right.' Panther said.

'Anant is in charge; he has all the secret information. Why don't you contact him? You know him since College days.' Posco said.

'Anant will never share sensitive information; he is against betting. He will throw me out if I talk to him about betting.' Panther said.

'I will work out something by tomorrow evening.' Sikri said.

He knew he would definitely be able to do something.

- - - - - -

Chapter XII

I was invited by my Alma Mater, St John's College Dharampur, to be the Chief Guest at the Annual Debate Competition.

The topic of the debate was whether betting on Sports should be legalized in India.

The students in favor of the topic said betting should be legalized, and it can be subjected to very high rates of taxation. This will be a source of revenue for the Government which can also regulate the activities and persons connected with betting. In any case, the authorities are not able to check the betting, and the unregulated betting falls in the hands of the underworld. The betting is legal in several Countries. In our Country also, betting on horse racing is legal in some parts.

The students speaking against the motion said betting is evil. It can lead to financial ruin. There are instances where people committed suicide after losing heavily. Some students steal money and lie to their parents when they get addicted to betting. Since betting is controlled by the underworld, it is associated with so many crimes. The most important point is that when one is placing bets on the basis of certain assumptions, one does not even know that the match or the spot may be fixed.

In my speech as Chief Guest, I advised students to stay away from all kinds of gambling and speculation.

'Students must participate in games and sports. They can watch sports on TV in their spare time, but they should never be under the notion that they can predict the outcome of a sporting event, or that they can make money by placing bets on the outcome. It is only the money earned through hard work and fair means that brings true happiness and glory.'

Then I asked all the students present in the auditorium to take an oath never to gamble or speculate in life.

- - - - - -

Chapter XIII

Sikri was waiting in his study for Posco and Panther. He was toying nervously with his laptop which would soon give him a couple of crore rupees.

It had taken seven days for Sudha to come out of depression after the emotional trauma she suffered at the breakfast table that morning at Kamal's Farm House. She was still feeling disconsolate.

Sikri knew Anant and Sudha were together in college, but he was not aware of their emotional entanglement. Anant's behavior that morning at the Farm House turned his thoughts in that direction.

Once she was her normal self, Sudha told Sikri everything about her emotional involvement with Anant. She told him that the affair was not one sided because Anant also loved her; he even used her name as password for his email account and secret files.

It did not bother Sikri much that his wife was emotionally involved with Anant. For him, Sudha was only a trophy; a beautiful, cultured woman to enhance his social standing. The important thing was discovery of Anant's password. Sikri knew from experience that people often stick to the same password, particularly if it reminds them of a college sweetheart.

He was spot on. By using Anant's account, he sent an email to Anant's CA (Chartered Accountant) asking him to mail copies of the files on team strategy. He was on cloud nine when he could access those files with the same password.

Sikri's machinations got him what he wanted.

Panther and Posco arrived shortly. The betting king Razaq was also with them.

Panther was carrying a brief case full of currency notes.

'Are we good?' 'Posco asked.

'Yes Sir.' Sikri replied.

'Here is your rokda (cash)' Panther said handing over the brief case to Sikri.

'Make good use of the information. You are not a team official, so you can place bets without any legal consequences.' Posco told Razaq.

'Man! You do not know me! Razaq kam karta nahi, karwata hai(Razaq gets things done through others instead of involving himself).' Razaq said.

OK, bye Sikri. Thanks a ton. Posco, Panther, and Razaq walked towards the door.

Suddenly, Sudha entered the study.

'I have overheard everything. I will inform Anant.' She said.

'You will do no such thing' Sikri said in a loud commanding voice.

Sudha took out her mobile phone from her purse. She was about to call Anant's number when a bullet hit her in the chest.

It was Razaq who had fired the shot from his revolver.

Posco, Panther, and Razaq vanished in thin air. Sikri was left with injured Sudha who was unconscious and bleeding profusely.

Sikri had the presence of mind. He called for ambulance and informed the Police that some unknown person fired a shot from the window, and that when he looked out the assailant was running away with his back towards the house; he could not identify the assailant because it was dark.

Sudha was admitted to the emergency ward. She was in coma and doctors said her condition was critical.

- - - - - -

Chapter XIV

B aldev was free that evening; he had packed up early because the unit wanted to celebrate Dusshera.

He desperately wanted to see his son; he thought about visiting Mala, but he did not have the nerve after the way he had treated her.

At this stage, he was deeply involved with Sayeeda. The intoxicating effect of a new relationship made him a great lover but a bad husband and father.

Sayeeda had become one of the top heroines, and Baldev was so much under her spell that he neglected everything else.

He ran out of his luck after Mala moved out of his house. His last two movies failed miserably, and the offers to direct new movies were dwindling. As Sayeeda wanted him to turn into a producer, he borrowed large sums of money from financiers and started making a very ambitious film with Sayeeda in the lead role.

Sayeeda's interference with the production made it very difficult to control the expenses, and the budget of the film was going out of hand.

Still, everything was fine till Sayeeda was with him. There was so much of woman in Sayeeda that even one evening with her was worth all the trouble. Baldev's judgment had become totally clouded by the charm of sensuous Sayeeda.

He asked Raju to take out the car with the intention of visiting Sayeeda; the thought that he would soon be with Sayeeda made him feel at the top of the world.

- - - - - -

Raju was driving carefully; he didn't want to lose a fat salary job with such a high profile master.

Just two days back, he had gone to Baldev's place looking for a job. Baldev recognized him immediately as Anant's driver during College days and employed him.

By another coincidence, Champa got job as cook and Santosh Junior's Aaya at Mala's place.

Baldev reached the imposing building in Andheri West where he had bought Sayeeda a flat. He knew Sayeeda did not have shooting dates for two days. He thought about calling her over mobile phone, but then he thought he would surprise her.

He pushed the bell. The door opened after almost five minutes which seemed like forever to Baldev.

Sayeeda was at the door. She was scantily dressed.

'Oh, it is you! Why didn't you call?' She said.

'It's a surprise, Babe'. Baldev said and moved towards her to take her in his arms.

Suddenly he realized they were not alone.

His arch rival Gautam was sitting on sofa.

Gautam was the top Producer Director of the time; grapevine had it that Sayeeda was likely to sign his next film. She had not yet worked with Gautam because Baldev did not like it.

During Baldev's struggle period, Gautam had insulted him. When Baldev became successful; he avoided Gautam completely. In filmi jargon, they belonged to different camps.

Since Sayeeda was Baldev's protégée, it was never thought possible that she would work with Gautam.

Gautam's presence in Sayeeda's flat enraged Baldev.

'Gautam! Get out of here.' Baldev shouted.

'I invited him. He wanted to discuss a project with me.' Sayeeda said. She was unruffled.

'Get out! I say.' Baldev again yelled at Gautam.

Gautam kept sitting on sofa with a roguish smile on his face.

Baldev moved towards Gautam, and tried to pull him physically.

Gautam was tall and muscular, while Baldev was lean and thin.

Gautam got up and slapped Baldev.

When Baldev tried to retaliate, Gautam hit him on face so hard that blood came out of Baldev's nose.

Sayeeda went inside to get the first aid box, but it was too late. By the time she came back to the drawing room, Baldev had left.

Raju took Baldev to Dr Shah's clinic; there was just one stitch, but Baldev's soul was wounded beyond repair.

- - - - - -

Chapter XV

Mala and Baldev's mother Asha were waiting impatiently outside the intensive care unit of the Holy Family Hospital. Champa stayed back as she was taking care of junior.

Baldev had consumed an overdose of barbiturates.

Raju had informed Mala over phone, and they all rushed Baldev to the hospital.

'Next 48 hours are crucial.' Doctor Shah said.

Mala and Asha had not slept the whole night. Now it was around ten in the morning.

Suddenly, the hospital lobby was full with reporters.

Sayeeda came to see Baldev at the Holy Family Hospital.

Since nobody was allowed to see Baldev, Sayeeda had to ask Mala about how he was doing.

Mala was endowed with equable temperament. She maintained a dignified silence.

More reporters and Sayeeda's fans filled the lobby, and it became very difficult to manage the crowd.

Suddenly, Baldev's mother Asha pounced on Sayeeda, and landed a juicy upper cut on her face.

Sayeeda was taken aback; she wobbled and almost fell down.

All cameras focused on Sayeeda. The reporters had a field day; this was even more sensational news than Baldev's suicide attempt.

Mala moved ahead and stopped Asha from creating further unpleasantness.

'Mummyji you go home and rest.' Mala told Asha.

Sayeeda thought it wise to leave.

Raju drove Asha to Mala's flat and came back with daily newspapers. They all carried the same headline about Baldev's attempted suicide.

Mala had barely finished reading the headlines when she saw Raju rushing to touch feet of a pale looking lady in her fifties.

It was Lata on wheelchair; she had come to Holy Family Hospital for dialysis.

- - - - - -

Chapter XVI

I was sitting with my grandfather in his house when Basant Uncle came to see him.

Basant Uncle was feeling very low.

Lata Aunty needed dialysis very frequently. Her kidneys were badly damaged; she needed a transplant.

For a family like theirs, there was no dearth of donors. Unfortunately, no profile matched and Basant Uncle was getting worried.

Things were not good at the family front either. Anant had left for an undisclosed destination after his CA told him about the email. He never tried to contact the family. Nalini and Diya went to live with Nalini's sister in Pune; Nalini was very upset with what had happened.

'I have full sympathy with you Basant. May Lord Ram bless you!' My grandfather said.

'I am devastated. I do not know what to do?' Basant Uncle said.

'Let us have faith in God Almighty. He always helps his true devotees.' My grandfather addressed to Basant Uncle's despair.

'You should organize Akhand Path (non-stop recital) of Ram Charit Manas.' Mohan will help you.' My grandfather suggested.

Then, my grandfather recited the following Doha from Ram Charit Manas.

"Brahm Ram Te Namu Bade Bar Dayak Bar Dani.

Ram Charit Sat Koti Mah Liye Mahesh Jiye Jani."

The above means that the name of Lord Ram is Superior to Brahm and Ram himself. This can bless even those who have the powers to bless others. Therefore, Lord Shiva has chosen the name 'Ram' out of more than a billion descriptions of the God.

- - - - - -

Chapter XVII

I contacted the local kathavachaks in Mumbai and organized a three day Akhand Path of Ram Charit Manas at Basant Uncle's residence.

Fourth day was 'Prasad'(offering) to which Nalini and Diya were invited among other relatives and friends. I had also invited Karan who was now posted as Deputy Income Tax Commissioner in Mumbai.

We had completed the Akhand Path, and were preparing for distribution of Prasad.

I got a call from Mala. She was ecstatic.

'Baldev has come out of coma! Doctors say he is out of danger.' Mala spoke over phone.

'You must come here for Prasad.' I said.

'Sure! Junior also needs to be blessed'. Mala replied.

Raju was driving the car. Champa was holding Santosh Junior sitting next to Mala in the backseat.

During the last seven days Raju and Champa had faced each other on several occasions, but each time Champa looked down and avoided eye contact.

Mala touched Lata Aunty's feet. Then, she moved towards Basant Uncle to touch his feet.

At that time, Nalini entered with Diya.

She moved forward and hugged Lata Aunty.

'You have suffered so much, and didn't ever speak a word to me about it.' Nalini said.

Lata Aunty was in tears. She could not speak.

'Dr Desai has told me everything.' Nalini said.

'I have got my profile tested. It matches yours.' Nalini added.

'You will donate a kidney to Lata!' Basant Uncle exclaimed.

'You do not have to do that.' Lata Aunty said.

'Anything for you, Ma.' Nalini said.

'Dr Desai has already consulted Dr Vyas, the Urologist; and set a date for the transplant.' She added.

'How is Baldev?' Mamaji asked Mala.

'He is out of danger. Doctors say they will discharge him after three days.' Mala replied.

'But he is neck deep in debt because of his incomplete film with Sayeeda.' I told Mamaji.

'Do not worry! I have already spoken with a producer who will take over the project and pay off the debt.'

Mamaji's words were like music to Mala's ears. She was glad that Baldev would be able to break Sayeeda's spell. She did not know how to express her gratitude to Mamaji.

She bent and touched Mamaji's feet.

'Don't be silly'. Mamaji lifted her and then embraced her.

At this stage, Champa entered with young Santosh in her Arms.

Basant Uncle, Lata Aunty, Mamaji and Nalini joined me in blessing the junior.

Young Diya also came up and gently stroked junior's head, who was now in Mala's lap.

And then, we witnessed a filmi scene.

Champa was lying prostrate at Raju's feet. She was crying and begging Raju's pardon.

Raju held Champa's hand and she got up. All was forgotten and forgiven; had we not been present, Raju would have taken Champa in his arms.

Basant Uncle's domestic help announced arrival of Karan. We all rushed to greet Deputy Commissioner Sab.

Karan was in good mood.

He told me how he helped Verma Sir and his son Bunty.

Verma Sir did not know what to do when Bunty ran away with the cash he had withdrawn for his surgery. He rang up Karan and told him everything. Karan co-ordinated with the local Police Authorities and got the bookie arrested. With the bookie behind the bars, it was safe for Bunty to come back home. Karan also requested his friend Dr Rana of PGI Chandigarh who operated on Verma Sir free of cost.

Mala's phone started buzzing; she jumped with joy when she took the call.

It was the doctor from the Medical College Hospital, Ramnagar.

Sudha had regained consciousness.

On Sudha's complaint Police arrested Sikri, Panther, and Posco; but Razaq had already fled the country.

Police seized Sikri's laptop, and it was established that Anant's email account had been hacked.

Anant was cleared of all the charges.

- - - - - -

Epilogue

It had been fifteen years since we graduated from St. John's, and a reunion was organized at our Alma Mater in Dharampur.

It is a wonderful experience to go back to the halcyon days of student life. Though many of us had developed pot bellies and receding hairlines, we thought ourselves to be the same young person we were in the College days. It was also an opportunity to see our College time friends in a totally informal atmosphere; some of them we were meeting for the first time since College. The pristine landscape and salubrious climate of Dharampur enhanced the feelings of bliss associated with the event.

One of the events of the reunion was the batch meet when, one by one, all the participants introduced themselves and their families.

Karan had not been able to come to the reunion because of an important official assignment.

Neelu was the first one to tell her story. Like in college days, she had a beatific smile on her face.

She told us she was married to a Gastroenterologist in Delhi who had a roaring practice.

Garima had married an NRI and was living in London.

There was a huge applaud when Mala, Baldev and Santosh Junior came up the stage. Baldev had regained his stature as top Movie Director. He was the main attraction of the event; a large number of fans had gathered in Dharampur to get a glimpse of him.

Mala was as charming as ever. She was dressed in style as befitted a Bollywood Film Director's wife.

After Baldev and Mala, it was Sudha's turn.

Sudha's appearance was demure though she had been the beauty queen during College days. In striking contrast to Mala, she dressed simply and was not wearing any make-up. She told us that she was now running an NGO to help the underprivileged children.

Then, I got up to give an account of what I had done in the last fifteen years.

Suddenly, there was a commotion and all eyes turned towards the gate.

A familiar figure entered the Hall. It was none other than Anant.

We all applauded heavily. There could not have been a more pleasant surprise.

I invited Anant to the stage.

After the cheer died down, Anant began to speak.

All of us were listening intently.

"Dear friends,

You must have heard so many things about me. Today I have come here to share everything with you.

This institution has given so much to me. I came to this College when I was passing through a difficult phase in my life. I found it difficult to concentrate on studies. My arithmetic sense was horrible and I hated paperwork.

I am grateful to my teachers and friends who molded me into a better human being. I sincerely apologize for my behavior on certain occasions, though I never meant any disrespect.

I am very sorry that because of my thoughtless actions, I hurt the feelings of some of my close friends who cared so much for me. I was so raw at that time that I could not sense my own feelings.

You might remember me as an over confident guy, but the fact is I was very insecure from within.

It was because of the positive influence of this institution and support of my friends like Mohan, Karan, Sudha and Mala that I slowly but surely improved. Initially, I used to take things for granted but then I realized I have to make efforts to find my place in the society.

I could never become a scholar, but I have always been an avid Sports lover. It has been the mission of my life to improve the Sports Facilities and to create better opportunities for the youngsters. My passion for Sports found a new meaning in this institution which shaped my destiny in the following years.

When I came in contact with the Sports Bodies I came to know that, though there are many good and well-meaning Sports Administrators, some persons become Sports Administrators only for power and lucre; and they are the ones who cause the greatest damage to the system. Unfortunately, I ran into the second kind and got disillusioned. I worked for a good cause, but I had to reap the whirlwind.

I went to the mountains to meditate. I have come back as a changed man.

I have decided never to associate myself with any formal Sports Set Up.

But I am not quitting.

I want to be the voice of the young Sports Aspirants; I will fight for the rights of the youngsters, and ensure that no injustice is done to them when it comes to Sports.

I will devote my time to coaching and counseling young Sports Aspirants. There is so much talent available in our country, but are we sincerely searching for the talent? Have we built enough playgrounds? Are we providing the right advice and guidance?

I will make available the right platform where the talent can show itself and get appreciated.

I request you to send your suggestions to my website Anant dotcom."

We all gave a standing ovation to Anant.

-----The End----